Chrysoula Georgoula
Call Me Stratos

First published by Vakxikon Publications, 2022, Athens, Greece.

The right of Chyrsoula Georgoula to be identified as the author
of this work has been asserted in accordance with the Copyright,
Designs and Patents Act, 1988

First published in 2025 by Istros Books London, United Kingdom
www.istrosbooks.com

The publishers wish to thank the Arts Council England.

Supported using public funding by
ARTS COUNCIL
ENGLAND

LOTTERY FUNDED

Chrysoula S. Georgoula

Call Me
Stratos

Translated
from the Greek by
MARIANNA AVOURI

istrosbooks

Part one

Chapter 1

It was that particular Sunday; or rather that damn weekend, when the shitshow started. The reason was those two cats Sotiria dragged in from her village, this hint of a village in the Ambracian Gulf. The family would get to catch some sun and go swimming while the arsehole, that's me, would hang a "CLOSED FOR VACATION" sign on the Tsunami Garage door, for the second year in a row, and work his ass off throughout August for eight grand.

"What is that, woman?" I kicked the carton that meowed on the floor.

"Two kittens, Strato, for the kids to play with," replied Sotiria.

Even though I can't stand four-legged creatures, I didn't even think to object. I'd be the last person to go against my wife's and children's wishes. And so, those two hairy devils settled in my house and kept getting in my way, snuggling under the furniture, meowing and pooing on the sofa. I put up with the situation for a week, the following one I take Sotiria aside and I tell her:

"Woman, four people and two cats in an 80sq.m. flat is too much. It's time for the four-legged creatures to take a hike so that the two-legged ones have room to breathe."

In the beginning, she played hard to get, laying out all sorts of random arguments, the kind that psychologists talk about on the morning shows: "Animals contribute to the socialisation of children and children that grow up caged in four walls, adore them..." and yet, after bargaining for an hour, we agreed to let one of the two go. I did her a favour that is, given that pets were a pain in the ass and she had already grown weary of them. Pets require care, money, vets, and we had neither the time, the desire, nor the money to spare.

That Saturday, Sotiria worked the night shift. When I finally put the kids to sleep (they always hit the sack after one o'clock), I managed to grab one of the two–the bastards slip through your hands like eels–and left it out into the street. Then I drank two glasses of scotch and fell asleep on the sofa until dawn, when I was woken up by meows coming from the balcony.

I go out and I see that the cat I had kept was hanging by the railing and the other one was stuck between a dustbin and the rear tire of a car, caterwauling. I kicked the remaining animal towards the lounge and shut the door, drank some water–my mouth tasted sour–and lay back on the sofa certain that the damn cat would quieten down, which it did. I tossed and turned, left, right, face down, added another pillow, rested my feet on the coffee table, lay with my head facing the balcony door and put my feet up on the kitchen hatch, where the three-seater sofa ends–all to no use. Didn't sleep a wink. I look at the clock on the opposite wall over the stereo. It was twenty to eight. Those beasts had screwed up my Sunday.

I got up with intense back pain and made a double frappé with three teaspoons of sugar. Then I cleaned the visible splashes from the tiles and the kitchen counter, lit a cigarette and lounged on the balcony to cool off. On the street, the leaves of the trees below were completely still. Every so often, at a few minutes apart, I could hear the bells of Saint Andreas', Saint Antony's and Prophet Elijah's, along with barking, and the noise of Dessie's nail clipper from across the street; Dessie who liked to clip nails, pluck eyebrows and talk on the phone with her friends on the balcony on Sunday mornings.

8

Sotiria was due to return at nine from the home for the elderly with Alzheimer's, where she worked as a nurse. The children were sleeping inside and my head was pounding. If one night I overdo it and drink one too many whiskeys, the next day I have a crazy headache, which doesn't go away unless I vomit. I'm growing old. Where have all those beautiful years gone, when I hung out with my mates and we roamed the pool halls and sleazy bars on Patission or the cafes in Saint Andreas' Square like cowboys, with a Marlboro hanging from our lips and a flat metal hip flask with whisky in the back pocket ... There goes youth, there goes beauty, never to return.

The cat came out meowing and stretched in front of me a couple of times as if it was doing gymnastics. It probably wanted to impress me, but I didn't fall for it, instead I went back to drinking my coffee without paying attention, until it started meowing again.

"Shut up!" I said angrily and it did. I lit a cigarette and just when the tobacco eagerly touched my lips, the cat lets out a shrill scream. Then the other one from downstairs begins to meow, with the shutters open, and it caused such a rumpus that I feel a surge of anger and, before I had time to think what to tell Sotiria and the kids, I hurled the hairy devil out the window, and saw it bounce twice and then land on the street three storeys down.

"What happened?" yelled Mrs. Dimitra who lived on the second storey.

"A cat. They threw out a cat!" Dessie stopped the pedicure and shoved her head under the awning.

"Who threw out the cat?" Mrs. Dimitra asked again.

"Someone from your block of flats," said Dessie and I saw her pointing at me nodding her head. I stormed in, left the balcony door ajar and pulled the drapes. Then I rushed into the bathroom to empty a bottle of surgical spirit on my hands that, despite washing, reeked of cat fur. Finally, I stood behind the curtains in the lounge and listened to the female neighbours, who were left horror-struck by what had happened to the cat.

Chapter 2

They say cats have nine lives and our cat was no different. From what I heard just before I went out like a light, it landed on the street unharmed, and with the help of the other cat and a compassionate girl from next door, found shelter in a rickety building nearby. Sotiria came home at about nine, but she didn't stop to listen to the conversations that continued from one balcony to the next, given that we don't even acknowledge our neighbours, such as they are. She rushed in as always and found me with the doors locked, fast asleep.

"Wake up, it's almost noon!" she shouted and took off her shoes–she walks barefoot around the house from winter to summer. Then she filled a cup with milk for the cat and opened the balcony door wide.

"There'll be no smoking in the lounge, we have children," she explained, while snatching the Marlboro which I was about to light as she passed by, calling the cat to no answer.

"Strato, do you happen to know where the animal is? I don't suppose you've ditched both of them?" she questioned and began searching for it behind the hatch, under the coffee table and the sofas.

In a somewhat confusing manner, I gave her the general idea of how I took the one downstairs and how the other one wouldn't let me sleep and I threw it off the balcony so I could get some rest and the things that Mrs. Dimitra from the second storey discussed with that mare, Dessie, from across the street...

"They saw you throw the cat onto the street?"

Sotiria was left, dumbfounded, with the cup of milk still in her hands.

"Agh! What have you gone and done, you pitiful man! Haven't you heard of that little prick in Kiato who was arrested because he doused a mutt in front of his store and received a thirty thousand euros fine? Let's hope you don't get sued, because we're screwed if you fall into the hands of the animal lovers/environmentalists!"

Flustered, she headed downstairs to look for the cats among the ruins. She found them next to a cup of milk.

"Who fed our cats?" her angry voice was heard all the way to the lounge.

"Your husband threw them off the balcony and since they failed to drop dead, my daughter nursed them," replied the prick who lives across the street on the third floor, one storey up from Dessie.

"Kittens happen to fall, no one did them any harm," Sotiria explained, and without paying attention to the prick, who kept on being a wiseass by saying that the cats had attempted suicide, she brought them back upstairs. Outraged, I grabbed them from her hands and didn't leave them in peace until the afternoon, when I took them to Tourkovounia hills, which was the beginning of another story.

I parked just before the Zepelin café and took a right through the pine grove that goes all the way up to the cliff. I held the bag of cats in one hand and the green metal shovel in the other, the one which Nickie digs holes in the sand with during the summer. I inspected the grounds and, just before the precipice, I dug a deep pit and emptied the beasts into it. They meowed with all their might and tried to latch onto the walls, while I was pushing them down with my shoe. They struggled to surface, once, twice, three times, until they got stuck and there was nothing else to do but cry. I took the shovel and covered them with plenty of dirt.

The sun had started setting and the solar panels were glowing all the way down to the sea that sat in Piraeus' lap. Going back to the car, I couldn't find my keys. I broke out in a cold sweat at the thought I had buried them along with the cats and that I'd have to uncover the pit. I returned to the crime scene worried and stressed. The sun had disappeared behind the suburb of Egaleo and muffled meowing was still coming from the freshly dug dirt. I take a look around in the dimming light and saw something shining under a bush.

"My keys!"

I crawled below the smell of fresh branches to get them and suddenly felt sick to my stomach. Shoving my head in the grass, I puked like crazy. As I was leaving, the meowing had stopped.

Ever since that Sunday, and Sotiria's cats, I realized my deep hatred for the smell of those animals that tear open discarded paper bags and litter the pavement with bones; for toilet paper and sanitary napkins soaked in black blood; for that smell of fish on the unwashed bodies of niggers all over the place; for the rot of morning mouths that talk incessantly about everything and for the stale hairspray that puffs up the curly hair of the ladies that exit my aunt Helen's hair salon, swaying their hips, with the certainty that a haircut and a hairdo has turned them into movie stars.

Chapter 3

The time it takes to smoke a cigarette is how far my house is from Saint Antoniou, where in the basement of my childhood home I operated my elite car wash and car polish business under the name of 'Tsunami'. Daily I covered the same distance on foot, except for that Monday, when I went down to the underground car park with the lift and, even though the fuel light had come on and I couldn't possibly afford to put in more, took the car and fled just before seven o'clock. And all because I wanted to leave before Mrs. Dimitra from the second floor, who leaves early to go to the fishmonger's at the end of Traleon, and Dessie, the bitch from across the street, who every morning prior to heading to her pool hall, shakes out her bedsheets and blankets over the heads of passers-by. I wanted to avoid an unpleasant encounter with them, knowing that if they said anything about the cats, I'd let them have it and it wasn't the time to get into trouble: I had a wife and kids to look after.

At five past seven I rolled up the right garage door of the Tsunami, turned on the pneumatic drill and picked up the wind-screen wipers and cleaning wads which I had dropped on the floor, hurrying to close on Saturday afternoon. Around eight, I climbed up on a stool at Paranda next door and ordered some coffee to wake me up while I stared at the traffic on Irakliou picking up as the day progressed.

At about nine, Stathogiannis double-parked his car in front of the Tsunami and came to hang out with me. Shortly after, Lola the waitress brought my coffee and took my friend's order.

"One freddo cappuccino with two teaspoons of sugar," said Manos half-smiling. The girl returned the smile and walked away with an arousing gait.

"Nice *equipment*," my mate said winking.

"You better not look at other girls' equipment, or you'll risk ending up outside the cemetery with a white cane," I said and went grumpily inside the Tsunami to wash his car, a 2002 Mercedes model.

"Have the Black Beauty ready by eleven. At twelve I'll be showing her off at an auction on..." A honk, an abrupt stop, and the swearing of two drivers coming from the avenue didn't let me hear whether he said Filis or something else. Filis, I think.

I was putting the key in the ignition when out of the corner of my eye I saw Labros' wife, who about two years ago I had persuaded to move the auto electronics repair out of the ground floor of my childhood home in order to open up the Tsunami. I turned the engine on and revved up so as to avoid listening to that jinxed woman wishing me good morning first thing on Monday morning when I just opened the shop. When I saw her in my rear-view mirror crossing the street with her dancing gait, I spat in my chest twice to ward off bad luck and slid the Mercedes into the automatic car wash machine. In an hour, it was spick and span inside-out. I left it on the pavement across the street glistening under the sun, which had risen slightly above the block of flats. For the time being, I couldn't tell if another client was coming.

On Mondays, when business was slow, I would give my assistant, Sakis, the day off, and saved myself ten euros. At eleven, I handed the keys to Manos, who was talking with the grocer, Mr. Stelios, about the match between AEK-Panathinaikos, and lounged in his place until noon, ogling Lola.

Chapter 4

Tsunami is semi-detached and on the other side my mum's sister, Helen, has a hair salon and next to the hair salon, at the corner of Irakliou and Saint Antoniou, is Paranda, the only business which managed to stay afloat from when Mr. Pantelis shut down his convenience store.

The shop changed hands two or three times before Koula and her husband bought it. As soon as they got it, they tore down the glass storefront facing Irakliou, opened a window toward Saint Antoniou, and put a deep green regal on the ledge, paved the floor with grey tiles, painted the walls pistachio green, and loaded the brand-new lacquered counters with shiny coffee-makers. Afterwards, they paved the yard with Karystos slates and called me to build a pergola unlike any other in the whole of Patissia. In the two corners of the small yard, I installed two metal poles that I lined with dark wood, the colour of mahogany. I coated the roof with red brick, fire red, and made two slimline benches that could each fit fifteen tall chairs. On the right side there was still room for eight chairs and two bamboo tables for those who spent long hours there, like myself, and the human wrecks who couldn't climb on the counter chairs. They liked the job I did and they paid me handsomely. In the end, they covered the sides and the front with a transparent tent, which they took down during the winter months. In the summers they placed five or six tables in the park opposite the street to perk up the neighbourhood. Everyone was pleased and clientele was guaranteed. Koula's husband would show up at the end of the day to cash-up. My mother's sister, Helen, who, as a hairdresser, was the first to hear the neighbours' dirty laundry, used to say he gambled all their money in private games arranged by Dessie, that obnoxious woman across the street, at the Blue Sky pool hall.

"Have you heard? At the café next door, they hired the Albanian's daughter as a waitress," my mother said to me one afternoon on the veranda, where we were having our coffee watching Mr. Stelios dusting the box with the fruit beneath the sign "Katerina Supermarket" on the other side of Irakliou.

"Who? That sad excuse for a girl with the eye gunk and the runny nose?" I asked, and I remembered the Albanian girl's straw-coloured hair as she went about the neighbourhood like a slimy rodent. Once, Stathogiannis and I had her cornered at the altar of Saint Antony's and we would have had our way with her, if it hadn't been for my aunt Helen who caught us red-handed when she came in to light a candle (she also had issues of her own with the Saint ever since that day). After the attack, Lola would see us and head the other way, and we would scare her by chasing her the way dogs chase cats. After secondary school, she disappeared off the face of the earth and reappeared about ten years later with two kids, one motorcycle, and a tattoo on the nape of her neck. Mrs. Nickie told me that she had gotten married and divorced, and I told her to mind her own business and not to get involved in Albanian matters.

For me to be able to place Lola in the human category, I needed to set up my own shop nearby, a couple of years later. Before long I forgot her descent and I started liking her as a woman–I mean, who wouldn't go for a piece like her?"

"Lately you've been staring at her a lot." Memos, my old schoolmate and neighbuour in my block of flats, caught me checking her out.

"I like her ass, the way it spreads like a loaf of bread over the seat of her bike, her long blonde hair that opens up like a net over the street as she drives up on Irakliou, against the flow of traffic, revving the engine as if she is riding a wild horse with the coffees and the juices in one hand, and the steering wheel in the other. I love that black thunder she has tattooed on her nape. I love everything on her. If I make the mistake and look at her more than I should, I have to circle the block three times in order to cool off. And I still haven't told her that I want to shag her."

"Does Sotiria, know this?" he asked with a smirk and reached for my cigarettes.

"Oh, of course not, I can't tell things like that to my lawfully wedded wife," I replied and grabbed the cigarette pack before Memos, who's been a freeloader since birth, takes hold of it.

Chapter 5

That Monday I made do with the twelve euros I got from Black Beauty, which I spent on coffees and cigarettes. No use going home, can't raise a child on that! Luckily, Sotiria had a permanent job–thank God for Alzheimer's–and I had managed to put aside eight grand which I made from working at the construction site in August. Needless to say, my mother also helped out, one could therefore say that we lived a comfortable life. From Sotiria's mother we expected nothing except hopes and prayers. The old lady was chummy with Father Dionisis and spent her time inside churches around vergers, sitting in at funerals, and memorial services, repentance and incense. It was certain that the priests would bleed her dry to secure her a place in heaven.

By the time September 2010 was on its way out, the money taps were turned off, and the economic crisis had started penetrating into people's pockets. Customers who used to bring their car to the car wash once a week, now came once in a fortnight or once a month–or never. I had lost a few families completely, like Dessie's, who hadn't stepped foot in the shop since last June, when I threatened that if she didn't keep her dog from the balcony, I would poison it. Her son wouldn't bring over his Smart Fortwo car either. June, July, September, I'm leaving out August, three whole months. I was keeping track. Stratos may take his time, but doesn't forgive. I was all ears to pick up any information on the illegal gambling she arranged at her pool hall so I could call the Tax Authorities on her when she least expected it. The bitch was on my case and was about to pay dearly for it.

That day I came home at around four. Sotiria was at work and the kids were at my mother in law's. I had lunch and a little before five I put *Karras* on the stereo and turned up the volume. I have a kick-ass machine; you can hear it from Irakliou all the way to Perissos. I made an iced coffee and went out on the balcony to enjoy the music and my lame neighbours fussing on their balconies. None of these pussies had the guts to come to me on the street and tell me that I bother them. There's only gossip going around, people complaining my loud music doesn't let a person get a minute's peace.

Around six I put on *Karnava* and then *Active Member*, which I did for no other reason than to show them I can appreciate quality. Come seven, I get inside Sotiria's old Cooper, which was practically left in the parking lot of the building across the street, turn the key in the ignition, but get nothing. So I gun the engine hard and get it started, I try to pull out, and the car goes dead. I get out of the car furious and all-sweaty. One car in the parking lot with an empty fuel tank, Sotiria took the cabrio to work, and the third car is a piece of junk. And then you have me, the guy who washes everyone's cars, driving around in the Peugeot 2. I headed down Traleon and took Irakliou on the left. I turned right on Saint Antoniou and I knocked on the glass window of my aunt's hair salon, as she was catering to an old lady's hair.

"Are you off to see your mother?" Helen came out to the door holding the brush in her hand.

"No, I'm going to IZO, to see the boys. Come and have a beer when you close."

"Close? My last appointment is at nine. I'll be done at ten-thirty. I won't be up for beers then," she said and rushed back to the old lady's hair.

Helen doesn't have any kids or dogs, but she works like a dog, every day of the week, except on Sundays, when she takes trips to monasteries with a crappy travel agency, ever since the bloom was off the rose and not even a male cat would look at her.

I glanced at the Tsunami and took the narrow streets to arrive at Ano Patissia. I then headed down Chalkidos and right before Podoniftis bridge I stopped and hung out at IZO. Stathogiannis came at about eight. He said he would treat us to drinks given that he did well at the noon auction. Half an hour later, Smaras showed up; he'd had a weird, nagging cough for some time.

"Go see a doctor, you prick," I told him yet again.

"I don't need a doctor; I need a gravedigger," he replied and coughed his lungs out.

I've been with Stathogiannis and Smaras since the first grade. We hung out at school, at the playground, at the pool halls, with the babes, through all the drunkenness, and the big adventures. It pained me to hear his lungs caterwauling with each breath and see him staggering; a man over six feet tall. Now he was just skin and bones and his face was the colour of ash. His eyes rolled as though you had stepped on his belly. He was ill, we all knew it–he himself knew it better than anyone–but he wouldn't go to a doctor.

"Did you hear me? Go see a doctor," I repeated.

"I don't like life, man. I want to die, don't need any kindness. The only thing I pray for is that I die standing on my own two feet. I don't have any kids or dogs, last year I buried my mother, never got to know my dad. No one is going to care for me, no one is going to miss me," he said, and his black eyes lit up like coal.

"Don't say that, Smaras. We are going to miss you, we're brothers." We hugged him and started tearing up.

At around ten thirty, Stathogiannis snatched the cigarette from his mouth and dragged him to his house on Orfanidou. I continued to drink and smoke with the guy from the kiosk who drank at the table opposite mine, until he said something disrespectful about Panathinaikos and I sent him packing. The shop-owner stood over me angrily and told me to make myself scarce. He didn't want people in his shop who caused trouble, like me, he said. I left without paying.

"Good riddance!" I heard him say on my way out, but I didn't turn around. I wasn't in the mood for fighting that particular Monday.

Chapter 6

It took about a dozen of stops to get to Ano Patissia just as the last train was passing, all lit up. While weak at the knees, I felt really tense inside. I passed by Saint Barbara and walking alongside the electric railway tracks, I entered the pedestrian zone and ended up outside the half-collapsed gate of the old Bodossaki factory. A dozen or so sleazeballs sat on the benches under the plane trees.

"Mister, give us a ciggy, will you?"

I did. They also asked me for a lighter. I gave that too. They also asked me for five euros. I told them to bugger off and I chased after them with an armful of bricks I pried loose from the factory's stone fence. They were gone soon enough. They talk tough, but really they're pussies. Kids nowadays are chickenshit and with time, they'll be at everyone's mercy.

I paused at the corner of Irakliou and Saint Antoniou and glanced at the shop and my mother's windows. The light of the television flickered from the rolled down shutters. She still hasn't gone to bed. Mrs. Nickie, the hero! I started walking up towards Olofitou. By twelve thirty I was putting the key in the front door of my block of flats, when I saw, through the entrance glass panes, a shadow approaching me. I opened the door and bumped into Anna, Memos' wife, who lived on the ground floor and was lugging a big rubbish bag.

"Good evening, love, how have you been? I haven't seen Sotiria for days," she said and tried to fix her cross-eyed gaze on me.

"And I haven't seen Memos for a while."

"Memos' been in the Dafni mental institution the last couple of weeks," she said almost in tears.

"In Dafni? Why? What happened to my mate?" I was upset.

"You may not hang out together lately, but you know better than anyone, that his liver and his lungs are ruined from the alcohol. He's in no shape to get a job or earn a day's pay! With the money I make from my job at the municipality we just scrape by. We barely make ends meet. The other day I confided to my dentist, who sent us to a neurologist friend of hers, who felt sorry for us and agreed to hospitalize him for a month, in case we manage to get a paper for Social Security. I tried everything to get him to go in, but now he cries and pleads with me to get him out, and I beg him to stay, on the off chance they grant him a pension."

I felt weak at the knees. My friend in Dafni! Though we had grown cold towards each another, I never meant him any harm.

"Go visit him, love, one of those days, and tell him to stay," Anna begged me.

"I will," I promised her and went inside the house feeling sad.

Chapter 7

All night long, no matter how hard I tried, I couldn't get Memos out of my head: our drinking, our hook-ups with the ladies, and our fights. And the more I weighed these things in my mind, the more the scales tipped in favour of the parties, the promiscuities, and the brothel-hopping, and not so much in favour of our big fight in the beginning of 2005, at the time of the great wave of unemployment.

After the Olympic Games, it was impossible to find a day's pay in the market and almost every day I had drinks with Memos. But on the night of Saint John's Day, we went too far and quarrelled about the bloody football. He said something nasty about Panathinaikos, I told him something nasty about Manchester-United and during the fight he kicks me hard in the nuts and I fell apart. I came to at dawn, I remember, to shaking and shouting. I forced open my eye, the one which wasn't clogged, and saw Sotiria hovering over me and smacking me.

"Wake up, you piece of shit! You've turned our house into a whorehouse. I work like a dog all night and you are out on the piss."

I tried to tell her a couple of times that it was Memos' fault and she told me to shut up. For an hour I watched her like a wet cat from the kitchen hatch picking up the glasses and washing the black carpet and the sofa cushions out on the balcony. What a remarkable woman my darling Sotiria was, and what a good housewife; how beautifully her bare feet squeaked on the freshly mopped and sparkling clean tiles! Upon finishing, she tapped the Airwick three or four times and the scent of night flower drove away that of stale beer.

It was two thirty in the afternoon when Sotiria came to bed, dead tired. I lay next to her and, though she pushed me away in her sleep, I tucked my head in her scented bosom and fell asleep in the safety of her tits, which were the size and warmth of the sofa cushions I had pissed on.

Part
two

Chapter 8

January 2005 was so warm that in the news we would see bleary-eyed bears searching for food on the streets and in the yards of houses in mountain villages. I woke up, I remember, late in the afternoon all sweaty. Sotiria wasn't really on speaking terms with me and I was wrecked. That good-for-nothing man, Memos, had messed me up big time.

Around seven, my mum arrived along with Nickie, who had just turned two, and when she saw me limping, she fell into my arms. "Daddy has a booboo," she said and sobbed, that cheeky little girl. When we managed to calm her down, she grabbed my hand and she wouldn't leave my side. Sotiria and my mother went out on the balcony to smoke a cigarette. No one smoked inside the house, even if it was ten degrees below zero.

I assembled the bricks that my little one brought me with one ear pricked up to the half-open window door. The two women were chatting quietly. I was certain they were badmouthing me. After a while they asked me to join them. I came out with the little one in my arms. Mrs. Nickie went all serious and told me it was about time I stop playing around. I was a man, I had a family, a house, and obligations, and it wasn't proper that the neighbourhood complains about the drunkard who quarrels with his mates, and won't let anyone get a moment's rest. Sotiria threatened me that if I kept this up, she would leave and take the kid with her;

and that is when I teared up and I swore that alcohol would never touch my lips again, I would cut ties with Memos and the rest of them and I would look for a job. But I wasn't to blame for being unemployed, I explained, Greece in general faced a nationwide problem. Ever since I was eighteen years old, I worked in construction without missing a day's pay, not to mention that I was the best roofer on the street. After the Olympic Games, though, there were no construction sites and nowhere to cast or install a roof. I was going to make an effort though, I promised. Stratos is not afraid of work, and I would absolutely work anywhere, and instead of using it to pay for beers, I would bring home the money.

The next day I woke up at dawn, as if I was headed to the construction site, and by eight o'clock sharp I was outside Taratselis' office on Saint Lavras. The first thing that comes to mind when I think about Taratselis is that late afternoon in the village one summer. I was on my way to the nests for eggs, when I heard a moan from my grandmother's barn. I see the cow along with five of our goats grazing on the last sunny part towards the street. Animals on the plot and moans in the barn! In the same place where the week before, grandfather Lefteris killed a sixteen feet snake that was eating the eggs with a double-barrelled shotgun. I was paralysed by the thought that my sweet-talking grandmother, who repeatedly scolded me for my so-called mischiefs, had sent me straight into the snakes' nest.

I tried to leave, but fear had my feet pinned to the barn's threshold with the door left ajar. I tried to scream, but no sound came out my narrow throat. As I stood there unable to move and frightened, I heard another moan, this one belonged to a woman. Two moans in the barn and some chatter I couldn't make out. The voice of Helen, my mother's sister, and the moan of the beast! I stick my head in and what do I see? My aunt in the nude, her legs wide open over the clover piles, and Nikos Taratselis, tall and erect in front of her, sticking it to her and both of them clucking like hens. I stood there with my mouth open watching them, until he let out an even bigger cry and pulled away. In between his legs, dripped a thick white liquid that wasn't piss.

With a sixth sense, I knew that what I'd seen was forbidden. I took off with my heart ready to burst. I told my grandmother that the nests were empty and she didn't believe me. The hens have been clucking all morning, she said and she was about to go to the barn herself, when my aunt came through the yard, all flushed, with her lap filled with eggs and her floral skirt ripped at the seam. "You lying brat!" said my sweet grandmother and before I had a chance to move away, she grabbed my ear and twisted it. I spent the afternoon killing every ant that happened to be on the ledge, while everyone else ate fried eggs with butter and warm bread.

Nearly two years after the barn incident, I came across Taratselis at the Antisteon coffee house in Kolokynthous, where I used to go with father on Sundays. Mr. Nikos was sipping his frappé while talking to my father about some construction. As soon as they finished talking, he gave me a 50 euro note–quite a lot of money back then. "Here, kid, get yourself a coke to drink," he said and gave me a friendly slap on the nape.

The first time I went to his office was with my mother when I finished high school. Taratselis had the same smile, but he had expanded as if he had been inflated with a pump. The only thing reminiscent of his physique back in the barn was his tall legs, that weren't as wide as the rest of his body. He was wearing an orange shirt and a blonde wisp of hair hung casually over his forehead.

"To what do I owe the pleasure, cousin?" he asked my mother from his big office.

"The university admission results came out today and Stratos didn't get in, anywhere. Well, since he's not going to be a scientist, as I hoped, I brought him to you to put him to work at the construction site, teach him the ropes, so he can earn some money.

This way I can catch my breath a little, because ever since my husband died, I've been fighting tooth and nail to make ends meet," my mother said and took the cigarette he offered her.

"Aren't you going to light one?" Mr. Nikos asked me.

"He doesn't smoke," my mother remarked.

"Who doesn't smoke?" He burst out laughing.

"Stratis," she said and glared at me.

"Do you smoke, boy?" Taratselis asked me, ignoring her.

"Yes, sir," I said and looked down.

"In that case, take one." He pushed the Marlboro pack towards me.

It was the first time I ever lit a cigarette in front of my mother, who nearly had a stroke, yet chose not to take things further. Taratselis agreed to take me on as a worker with half the wage and half the national insurance contributions, until I learnt the job.

"Tomorrow, boy, at five to seven be at the corner of Irakliou and Saint Lavras," he said to me at the door.

From that next day onwards, he had me carrying bricks and mud for his father, who was nearing seventy. I couldn't keep up with the old man. In the blink of an eye, he would erect an entire wall and he always shouted at me: "Stratos, the bricks, Stratos, the mud, Strato, move." I worked my ass off that summer, but I became one of the best bricklayers around. When autumn came, the roofer Theodoros, who paired with my father all those years, took me to work with him. Working next to them for two years I became one of the top handymen around by the time my deferment from military service had expired.

That's what I was reminiscing about when Mr. Nikos came that day.

"Well, if it isn't my nephew," he said and opened his office door with the two safety locks. He ordered me an iced coffee with three teaspoons of sugar. He hadn't forgotten how I took it! "What brings you here?"

"I came to get a day's pay, sir. I can no longer sit around, and I have problems with the family. My wife yells, my mother nags and my little girl wants new shoes."

"I got nothing." He shrugged his shoulders.

"For the others, maybe. But not for Stratos. Half the houses of the Olympic Village are there because of me, you must find me something to do. I got a wife and kid, and a loan to repay. After all, you're my mother's cousin." I appealed to his better nature, and he gave me twenty days' worth of pay at a villa in Ekali.

Like Saint George, with the cigarette puffing in his mouth and his hand on the wheel of his BMW, Nikos Taratselis once again offered me a way out.

Chapter 9

And so, we managed to overcome yet another crisis and I was back on the straight and narrow; a shiny example of a family man. From home to work and from work to home. I didn't see Memos any more, but I could smell him in the lobby of our block of flats and the more I sensed his breath close by the more I would turn into a raging bull given that he hadn't even bothered, that no-good bastard, to ring my intercom buzzer in order to find out what happened to me after he had left me unconscious that early morning. The lasting pain I still felt when I pissed and the fact that I could see the bruise on my left leg go from black to blue, then green, and finally yellowish, made my blood boil.

One morning I run into Annoula, his wife, on the street and raked her over the coals: "Shame on your man for reaching the point of hitting his best friends below the belt; he's a disgrace."

"The night of the fight, Memos was blind drunk and didn't understand what he was doing," she said under her breath, avoiding eye contact.

"If your dear Memos hadn't fouled his own nest, he would knock on my door and wouldn't play dead." Anna responded that he was my friend and that I should meet him in the middle.

I didn't answer back, I just walked away, angry. But my mind was set on getting back at him. I was working and all the while contemplating revenge; whenever I talked, I thought of him. Until two months later, on a Tuesday afternoon in mid-March, as I was smoking on the balcony pouring down half of the Jack Daniels bottle that I had planted in the big flowerpot containing the Ficus belonging to my wife–who turned out to be an environmentalist on top of an animal lover–a great idea hit me, one I would soon put to use.

Sotiria was making French fries and the cooker hood fan was working to the maximum. The kid was glued to the television, watching Mafalda. I took the opportunity to hide my caller ID on the cellphone and call 999 to report that Memos Papadogiorgas, who resided on the ground floor of Olofitou something, was actually a terrorist! "I realise that by making this accusation I put my own life on the line, but it wouldn't feel right if I left those family men at the mercy of a dangerous anarchist. I have reason to believe that he has a dozen Berettas and thousands of bullets hidden in his flat," I said and hung up.

After running up and down the porch a few times to take the edge off, I went to the kitchen, put five ice cubes in a glass and let my wife pour in a drop of the good bottle of whisky, as we had agreed. Afterwards I lounged on the bamboo armchair on the porch and watched the spring clouds as they chased one another like crazy across the sky.

I was feeling drowsy, when I heard the braking of a heavy vehicle coming from down in the street. I lean over the railing and what do I see! About twenty black-clad men jumping out of the side doors of two armoured black vans, armed to the teeth and moving into position from Traleon up to Ioannou Foka. The tallest one gave instructions with sharp signals, like a road traffic controller. Less than five minutes later, we heard glass breaking on the courtyard and a huge rumpus on the ground floor. From Anna's screams I figured that the coppers had gone into her house. Even today, I still can't explain how the coppers came so quickly, when you dial 999 to tell them you're being slaughtered and by the time they come you're already a corpse. Apparently, the word terrorism excites them.

"Strato, what's happening down there?" Sotiria came out with a cigarette in her mouth.

I pretended not to hear and sunk even deeper in the armchair, and went on enjoying that bloody water-whisky.

"Did you hear me?" Sotiria blew the smoke in my face.

"Did you say something?" I gave her a phony look.

"What are you, deaf? Can't you hear Anna's screams and Memos' swearing from downstairs?"

"They're probably fighting... Who knows what this angelic guy, Memos, has done again. Your best friend is in a pretty pickle for getting involved with such a deadbeat. But why should we care what they do? Fuck them!" I said.

"How can we not care about Annoula, who babysits for us when we have nowhere to leave the kid and won't take a dime? Despite her poverty, Anna is the only person who's on our side in the neighbourhood."

"She may be the best person in the world, but she is married to an asshole the likes of Memos. We shouldn't be involved with them. How about we take Nickie and head to the playground right now?" I said out of the blue.

"The playground, at this hour?" Sotiria wondered.

"Why, what's wrong with that? It's not even nine yet."

"What's gotten into you now? When have you ever taken her to the playground?"

"I think we should hit the playground and then go down to Hara for some *ekmek* ice cream."

"I don't know what to tell you..." she looked at me funny. "Any way, I'll go get dressed."

"No need to change. You look fine, my amazon." I looked at her legs spilling out of the crotch of her washed short trousers and gave her a slap on the butt.

"How about you? Will you be wearing the flipflops?"

"Why, what's wrong with them?" I said and I got hold of Nickie and walked out the door.

In the lift, Sotiria removed the kid's bib, who was screeching because I tore her away from the television. We could hear swearing and noise coming from downstairs as if the house was being gutted. We reached the ground floor and as we opened the lift door we stumbled upon the barrel of a gun of a black-clad copper in a hoodie.

"Eek!" uttered Sotiria frightened, and Nickie started crying.

"Why are you acting this way? Haven't you seen a copper from EMAK Special Forces before?" I said to my wife.

Nickie was pointing with both hands at the exit and Sotiria, who had gotten over the initial shock, was asking the copper what had happened.

"Don't ask questions and mind your own business," he said with a Rambo-like voice.

"You can't be serious! I'm not supposed to ask what's going on inside my own house?" Sotiria was staring at him, her face all flushed.

"Go, madam!" he said sternly, and as we were coming down the three small stairs, one step before the exit, all hell breaks loose and Memos' door opens and Anna comes out to the hallway.

"Sotiria, Strato," she runs towards us, with her hands open wide and her eyes welled up with tears.

"What is it, Anna love?" my wife turned back, oblivious of the copper who was yelling for us to leave.

"Go inside, madam!" the cop ordered Anna, and stood amid the two women.

"I will, Officer, but let me first talk to my friend and then I'll go get my husband's shoes. I don't suppose you're going to take him to the precinct barefoot, right?" Anna wiped her hands in her patched-up apron and opened the shoe organizer that they had put in next to the staircase, despite the decisions of the general meeting of the block of flats to keep it inside their frigging flat.

"What happened, Anna dear?" Sotiria disregarded the copper and hugged her.

"Well, Memos was asleep and I thought of making that blasted cake I was telling you about. As I was beating the eggs, I heard footsteps outside Mrs. Dimitra's parking lot and when I poured the vanilla in the bowl, I thought I saw someone's shadow behind the Leyland in the courtyard. I turn around and what do I see! The window is broken, shards of glass are in the dough and on the floor, and the copper is on top of the sink aiming a gun at me. I ask what's going on and he points his gun to the kitchen door, where two or three others were standing and motioned me to open it. I jumped over the glass, and unlocked it.

"Where is the terrorist, Memos Papadogiorgas, hiding?" One of the guys shoved a paper from the Public Prosecutor in my face.

"Memos, a terrorist! Are you sure you heard well, Officer?" I started laughing.

"The copper said someone reported that Memos is a dangerous terrorist and he advised me to be mindful when speaking to the police."

"Memos, a wanted man!"

"Where is your husband, madam?" he started yelling.

"You want my husband? Come on in," I said and went on to the hall. The coppers followed me hopping left and right like frogs with their backs against the wall. I opened the bedroom door and they saw Memos in his knickers sleeping soundly. They searched wardrobes and sofas, they threw our clothes out of drawers, they looked under the bed, they pulled out the bedside tables, and when they found nothing, they told me to wake up the suspect in order to question him."

"Not another word out of you, madam!" interrupted an officer with stripes who just came out of her flat.

"What is there to say, Officer? I'm just pouring my heart out to my neighbours, these good people who care about what happens to us."

"Who are these people?" he asked.

"The neighbours, Officer."

"Don't they have names?" he asked again bitterly.

With Nickie in my arms, I tried to push the door and get away, but found two more guys blocking my way.

"They are..." Anna looked at us desperately, "go on guys, speak. They are Sotiria and Stratos Achtidis from the third floor, good guys and good neighbours."

The copper advanced on me like a tiger.

"Huh, so you're Stratos Achtidis?"

"Yes, Officer."

"You 're the one who made the complaint?"

"What complaint are you talking about, Officer?"

He pulled a piece of paper from his pocket and upon glancing at it, he asked:

"The number 698xxx8332 belongs to you, according to the identification of the mobile telephone service. Isn't this the number you called us from to report that Memos Papadogiorgas is a terrorist and hides arms in his house?"

"It wasn't me, Officer. Someone played a joke on you."

"You know what's the sentence and the penalty for playing a joke on the police and especially the Counter Terrorism policing?"

"No, Officer, and I don't care."

"We'll see about that in a bit, down at the police station," he said, and it made my blood run cold. Sotiria, furious, grabbed the screaming kid from my arms, and got into the lift. I tried to follow her, but the copper tripped me and before I fell down, he grasped my arm and twisted it, and though I have a high tolerance to pain, I barely kept myself from groaning.

"You did all this?" Anna's sour breath was in my face. "Have you no shame, you lousy man? You tried to get Memos in trouble? Memos, with whom you've been through thick and thin together? Shame on you, you low-life, you bastard!" she said and spat at me across the right eyebrow.

I came close to fainting. I'd rather she sliced me with a razor than what that cunt did to me. If it weren't for the copper holding me back, I would have torn her to pieces. I wiped the flob with the back of my hand and wiped my hand on my blue short trousers, and started breathing through the mouth so that I don't smell her frigging saliva, which was stuck on me like glue. Anna took Memos' shoes and went inside her house with the Officer, and I was left with my back to the wall in the company of the two coppers.

After a while the door opened and out came about a dozen of them, armed with guns. Memos was staggering between them in his freshly ironed shirt and grey trousers with the crease, with a straight wet parting on the left and blurry vision from the drinking. I hadn't seen him since the day of the quarrel. The coppers took us by the arms and loaded us onto a van through the sliding door on the side. They made us sit facing each other. We didn't so much as exchange a look. Anna stood in front of the door; with her cross-eyed gaze shifting from one to the other, nodding her head. Then she turned to the copper.

"What happens now, Officer? Who will pay for the damage? Who will repair my broken window?"

"That gentleman over there," he said.

"He doesn't have a penny to his name. He owes to the bank; he owes money everywhere. His mother, his mother-in-law and his wife are the ones who support him. Expecting him to pay means that my house will be left without a window, and they'll be cats and Albanians coming and going as they please. Since you broke my window, you should pay for it."

"We'll see what we can do, madam. I'll send for the window-fitter who cooperates with the agency. We simply performed our duty. As for them, we'll take them to the police station to give their statements."

"Take them, Officer, take them and keep them, if you can, until late. To give me ample time to tidy up and make the blasted cake again," said the old bat and went inside without turning to look at us again.

That's what Annoula said. I rue the day I let her and her husband into my home. Ever since we were kids, Memos and I were in the amateur football team together, he was centre and I was forward. After secondary school, he disappeared off the face of the earth, and he turned up out of the blue, the day we moved to Olofitou.

"Strato, are you the new tenant on the third floor?" Memos hugged me.

I almost didn't recognize him.

"Where have you been all these years, my friend?" I asked him.

"I'll tell you," he said, and snatched the bedside table out of my hands.

When we brought the stuff up to the flat, I treated him to some whisky. Memos had a black thunder tattoo on his left arm and claimed to be a Manchester United fan. He said that after secondary school he went to work as a seaman. But don't think of Memos as a captain or a radio operator. He was hired as deck hand on a tanker that travelled from Liverpool to Dubai to Shanghai and all the way to Bangladesh, where he fell ill and was sent back to Greece half-dead; which made him think twice before setting sail again. By the time I found him in Olofitou, Memos was running deliveries at the vegetable market in a beaten-up van and was involved with Annoula; in her presence he acted like the Lord of the Rings instead of some bird dropping on the wrinkled collar of the world.

From that day on we chummed up with each other, our wives did likewise. When Nickie was born, Annoula offered to babysit when my mother couldn't. In the afternoons when Sotiria was working, I would call Memo upstairs and we would drink until his wife came to collect him. Those were good years... The construction business was booming, we had jobs and our pockets were full. Almost every week, we would head down to the venues that played island music on Acharnon, where Memos would request *"Eyes like yours are not to be found in the world"* and he would dance to it with Annoula who limped and was so cross-eyed that when she would glance at the table, she'd see the door. He was great to hang out with, obviously. Apart from telling him off when he farted and burped, me and Memos had no other dispute prior to the big fight.

Chapter 10

At the police station we were dumped like empty sacks onto two wooden chairs, in the presence of a copper. A desk next to the open window, three chairs–two chairs on which we were sitting and one behind the desk–as well as a coat stand behind the door, where a service cap hung, made up the entire furnishings of the long narrow room with the unpainted walls and the chipped mosaic floor tiles; a shambles. The copper was on the phone. On the desk, next to an old blotter, smoke was coming from an ashtray filled with cigarette butts. The copper glared at us and, without pausing, he motioned us. We didn't understand what he was trying to indicate, so we just sat and watched him in silence. From the moment we met at the entrance of our block of flats, this was the first time Memos and I exchanged looks.

The copper lit a cigarette and kept on talking about the chitterlings he used to eat at a souvlaki place on Irakliou whenever he worked nights. He then tugged at his shirt which left half of his belly exposed and, as if we weren't there, he went on talking about some woman named Margarita.

"They recommended her to us as a registered nurse, when my mother-in-law was in Attica General Hospital with a broken leg. We were pleased, I'm not saying otherwise. She was meticulous and knew her job well, not to mention she was asking for half the legal rate. The old lady, who hated everyone's guts, had only good things to say about the way she turned her on her side, made her bed and fed her. When she got out of the hospital, we took her home with us so she could look after our nuisance. That's how Margarita moved into the family home and I–who was always coming and going bringing them groceries and medicine–took pity on her and got her a residence permit, but only after she put out. Sometime later, having gotten used to this cushy lifestyle, as a thank you, she took off taking all of my gifts to her, the old woman's loose change and a cell phone! Can you believe that, man? She fled!" He banged his hand on the desk.

We were listening with our eyes fixed on the mosaic floor.

"And for what? She was under the impression that I had–listen to this–harassed her daughter, who in the meanwhile had moved into the old woman's house. And I told her that I never wanted to lay a hand on the girl; she asked for it and she loved it! And that's when the cunt mouthed off to me, saying it was a sin, that the girl was twelve years old and that she was going to leave. I couldn't take it so I raked her over the coals. The Albanian girl was too young, says she! Really? I'm going to get her, I will! I'll shag them both and then I'll put them on the bus in Omonia and send them straight to Kakavia. That will show that ingrate not to bite the hand that feeds her!"

That's what the copper was saying without minding that everyone around could hear him.

"Way to go, Officer!" I stood up and gave him a military salute when he hung up the phone. He shot me a vicious look and he told me, as he put out his cigarette, that he didn't care for my compliments and that I'd better shut up and try to figure out how I was going to get out of the mess I've made for myself. My blood froze.

A few minutes later they notified him to take us to the sergeant's office, where according to him we would get the third degree. So much for an interrogation. They shined a light onto our eyes and told us to confess. I told them I was playing a joke on my mate, simply to pass the time. Memos told them I was telling the truth. They created a case file against me, and big deal; I couldn't care less. With this and that, they let us go at around midnight and we returned home arm in arm, because after the interrogation we went by IZO to have one beer which by three o'clock had turned into a dozen. Blood is thicker than water.

Chapter 11

Come Wednesday at the crack of dawn, I left Memos on the ground floor scratching the door with his keys, and went up to the third storey on foot so as not to wake up Sotiria. At night one could hear the cables of the lift seemingly grazing our bedroom's wardrobe. I made it to the third storey with my tongue hanging out and a pain in my chest. I paused at the landing, blowing my breath into my palm and sticking it under my nose. I was clean.

I fumbled in my pocket for the keys and went weak at the knees. It'd be funny if I didn't take my keys, the way I left in such a hurry in the afternoon. Luckily for me, I found them in my rear pocket. I left the flip flops on the mat and opened the door taking every precaution. I closed the door and tiptoed left, towards the lounge. I stood still for a moment next to the hatch breathing gently. Not a peep from anyone.

I threw my clothes on the sofa, that were drenched in the stench of cigarettes and alcohol, had a glass of water and made my way to the bedroom. The door leaned ajar, the bachelor's dog from the floor beneath sounded hoarse. I pulled open the door with the light turned off and sat at the edge of the bed that made a creaking sound. Oh, my poor, suffering body. I lay down slowly and stretched myself out, reaching over to Sotiria's side. But she wasn't there! I had told her that the child needs to get used to the dark and sleep by herself in her room until I was blue in the face, yet once again my wife had slept with the child. It was our only fight regarding that child, and my sole demand. But with Sotiria it went in one ear and out the other. All her life she did as she pleased.

With the pain in my chest building up, I got up and went to my little girl's room. But the bed was empty too!

"Sotiria! Sotiria, where are you?"

I shouted and the fat-faced dog from downstairs answered me. Discouraged, I went to the lounge and turned on all the lights. I went out onto the balcony. The street was sloping down gloomily towards Traleon, occasionally lit by the headlights of some passing car. As far as my eyes could see, the blocks of flats were dark. So I get back in and being barefoot and all, I step on something. I start cursing, but I stop when I realize that nailed to my foot was the red door of Nickie's tiny Porsche.

I cracked open an ice-cold Amstel and stepped out onto the balcony, feeling its foam bubbles tickling my tongue and throat and easing the pain in my bleeding soul. It will pass, I reckoned, and lit a cigarette. The sky was dreary. I rested on the bamboo sofa and tried to relax. Where could Sotiria be now? Where is my child? If the missus has started sneaking out, we're screwed, I thought. I probably dozed off for a while, but the chill didn't let me fall asleep. I looked at the clock behind me on the lounge wall: 4:00AM. What do we do now, I asked myself. How do I get through the night?

I lit another cigarette and cracked open a second beer. It was Wednesday early morning and I hadn't secured a day's work. On Sunday, when I stopped by Taratselis' office to get paid, I learned that he was about to start a construction job at the end of Acharnon, but that he had assigned the formwork to Armouris, a toerag from Arcadia. "However, the roof is yours, since there's no better roofer in the whole Attica basin," he explained and again marveled at how, with all that drinking, all my roofs were level and how I hadn't so far come crashing down from seven storeys high, for the world to get rid of me once and for all; amused by his cleverness and blowing his smoke in my face. I came really close to telling him to bugger off.

It was a quarter to five and the three Amstel beers on the balcony table scattered their red metallic reflections in the half-light. As I watched them dancing brightly in front of me, I felt my body being carried away by their rhythm and the colourful pinball machine inside me turned on all the lights, releasing an insane cheerfulness that spread through my body like a warm and rumbling river which climbed upon my chest and my brain. *"Yannis dear, why is your handkerchief soiled..."*

I felt stuck, until my eye fell on the stereo to the right of the balcony door. How had I not thought about it sooner? Why hasn't the idea of throwing my own party occurred to me all this time? It's a shame to waste such high spirits. "Time to show off my 10-bit machine!" I tapped my head with my hand, lit a cigarette and, half-dancing, half-singing, I put on the CD with the songs from Epirus. *"I get dizzy, dizzy, when I think of you."* I cracked open a fourth beer, turned the volume up to eight and started dancing in zigzags. Getting drunk felt so good. The smell of beer crept sweetly into my nostrils and a shining dizziness burst into thousands of fireworks in my head as the whole place started spinning around me. The red ball of the pinball bobbed up and down inside me, joyful and mischievous, "tap, tap." I sang *"I get dizzy, dizzy, when I think of you, I get dizzy"* and swallowed a big gulp.

With a crooked cigarette in my mouth, I went out and clamped onto the railing with hands like claws. My muscles tensed to the point that the sleeves of my shirt creaked, about to rip. By the second song, *Yiannis' Handkerchief,* I was jumping for joy. Let's rock! let's rock! The balconies across the street began to light up one after another and I rushed to put the Scorpions on at full blast. "*Still loving you.*" Oh, Sotiria, what will I do without you; for a moment I felt a bit of tightness in my chest. Sotiria, you dumped me for no good reason... I teared up as I went out onto the balcony, where a laser beam hit me in the eyes and blinded me. Immediately, I push the off button and duck under the tent to the side, and I see the copper from the third floor across the street and confirm that he was the buzzkiller with the laser.

"I'll rip you to shreds if I get my hands on you, you bloody copper, for shooting that contraption into my eyes!" I motioned *fuck off* with my middle finger. He rose from his plastic chair and came to the railings in his white breeches.

"Are you talking to me?" he asked.

"Do you see another copper around here?"

"I, sir, I'm not a cop," he said with an infuriating calmness. "And, please, turn down the stereo."

"I know you're a copper and you're going to call the police. But now that I know my way around the police station, I don't care. I know how to calm those fellas down."

"I'm a civilian and I don't intend to call the police. Nonetheless you must turn down the music. It will soon be daylight and we have to get up and go about our jobs."

"What jobs, mister?" I asked laughing. "Do you know it will be more than five months since I've had an actual job? Do you know that today my wife left me? For that alone I have the right to throw myself a party!" I banged my hand on the railings.

"Do whatever you like, but don't ruin our sleep," said the pyjama-man and leaned back in his chair spreading his feet on another, barefaced mocking me. If I could reach him, I'd whack him a couple of times over the head, just to teach him not to act like a smartass.

I went into the lounge in a bad mood and I put on Nickie's Smurf songs at full blast. "*Smurfing Saturday, Saturday, Sunday...*" the walls trembled. I went out and I looked up and down the street all the way to the avenue. Almost every single block of flats was lit where before I started the broadcast, they were all pitch black. On the pavement, the Albanian woman who stayed in one of Mararas' rooms across the street (they hadn't yet offered that ramshackle building in return for financial compensation) was banging a large pot with a ladle. I turned down the machine and I kept on looking at her.

"Turn it off," she said, in a semi-Albanian, semi-Greek lingo. "We want to get some rest so that we can go and do our jobs bright and early tomorrow."

"What are these jobs you want to go to? The ones you snatched up from us and made us slaves instead of bosses? We were at the top of the heap before you came here."

"What are these jobs that you're talking to me about? Do you know many Greek women who wipe old people's arses or many Greek men who pick the olives for twenty euros per day?" the Albanian woman mouthed off to me.

"You shouldn't be here, you piece of trash. If you want peace and quiet, go to Albania. You daft cow! Now listen to this and learn," I said as I rushed to put Active Member on, but I was brought to a halt by the azure reflection of a police car siren on the balcony's roof. I turned down the stereo and sat on the sofa with anxious impatience until the bell rang. I didn't open the door. All of sudden I felt tired. It took a while before they rang again. I didn't answer, and went out instead and pretended to gaze indifferently up and down the street. From the opposite pavement they shone their flashlights on me.

"Sir, tell us your name, your floor, and let us in," a police-woman shouted at me, who from what I could tell–their flash-lights were blinding me–was easy on the eye.

"I'm not telling you my name nor am I letting you in," I responded, and they left. Just like that. As soon as I saw the police car turn onto the avenue, I put on *Karra* at full blast and brought the neighbourhood back to the railings. "Oh, Sotiria, what have you done to me... Taking Nickie with you..."

I lit one of her cigarettes and at the first puff the happy pin-ball machine turned its lights back on and the fuchsia ball started moving up and down in my guts, devouring the sudden fatigue and sadness. That is when the door opened and my frantic mother walked in.

"What's the matter son, what's wrong?" She threw the keys on the kitchen counter and, all hot and bothered, strode towards the stereo.

"Sotiria took the kid and left, and I, I'm having a party all by myself, mum."

"What are you talking about, child?" She turned off the stereo and stood there gazing at me sadly.

"Hands off the stereo, mum," I said and moved towards her.

"Child, why do you have to rattle people up? Why do you drink? Why do you cause me pain, my son?" She started crying.

"Who did I hurt, mum?" I asked and again sensed the weariness in my feet, weighing me down like lead.

"The gentleman," she pointed to the pyjama-man across the street.

"Who? Him? Can't you see, mother? The gentleman is enjoying himself," I said and leaned back on the sofa, drowsing off.

I woke up with the acute smell of Ajax for floors in my nostrils and a bloody headache lodged right between the eyes like a jellyfish. I turned to look at the time, but the light made impure by the double portion of ammonia, blindfolded me. I rose with difficulty. My bones ached and creaked. With squinty eyes, I held onto the ledge of the hatch and walked towards the kitchen. I felt my feet slip on the freshly mopped tiles and heard my mother shouting from the other room to stay put until it was dry. I flopped back onto the sofa. From the kitchen came the pungent smell of freshly brewed coffee.

When the floor dried off, my mother forced on me, despite my protests, to take a sip of coffee. I puked my guts out to the point of vomiting blood. The tearful Mrs. Nickie took a wet towel to clean the floor, the sofa, and my holiness, completely bladdered as I was. As I watched her hunched over me like that, I started feeling wronged.

"Oh, Sotiria, how could you take our flower and leave..."

I grabbed the cordless phone from the hatch behind my head and called my mother-in-law three times, but she hung up on me before I had a chance to ask to speak to my wife. That frigging caller ID.! I slammed the phone against the wall and shoved my head under the cushion. In about an hour, my mother decided to let me be. Before she left, she made sure there was no trace of alcohol in the house and made me swear I wouldn't drink any more.

"Okay, mum, okay. I'll see you tomorrow. Stop bugging me now," I said, closing my eyes.

Chapter 12

The afternoon was spent listening to children's songs. Just before sunset, Memos knocked on my door. His breath reeked of greasy dirt.

"Hey, man, don't you ever brush your teeth? Do you know what a toothbrush looks like?"

He thought that the curse words were a compliment and proudly flashed his hollow teeth at me.

"Shall we go to Blue Sky to get a beer?"

Blue Sky in in the corner of Traleon and Acrothone. You go down three stairs and fall right into the green world of billiards, with the hat-like light over each table and a strip of half-light on the floor, which doubles when it meets the half-light of the adjacent table, with the sound made by two or three balls colliding, the thump of the lucky ball that falls unsuspectingly in the dark black hole, with the fuchsia fruit machines that fluoresce at the lower right-hand corner next to the two bare tables that, when the curtains are drawn and the sign which says "Closed" turns to face the street, put on a green felt cloth and become the battlefield, where fortunes change hands leaving the profit of illegality in the pockets of Dessie and Takis, Mararas' oldest son, who are positioned behind the bar's counter, smoking like chimneys and serving us a bad whisky and beers, sulking, as if we've done something terrible to them.

"I'm not saying no to a beer, but I'm skint."

"Never mind, I got it," said Memos and pulled out of his pocket two crumpled fifty-euro notes.

"And where did you get all that money, you nitwit? You usually fail to see it when it's right under your nose."

"I combed the whole house and came across Anna's stash. Guess where that bloody woman keeps her money!"

"In the freezer," I said.

"No."

"In the kitchen, in between the pots."

"No. You are not going to find it."

"Just tell me already, you prick." I give him a friendly punch in the stomach.

"In one of her friggin' balls of yarn. I had to unravel a dozen of them, and right when I had given up hope, I found the dosh in the last one. Even that full-fledged Counter Terrorism unit you brought in couldn't locate that. Let's spend them on drinks before she catches us in the act and takes it away from me." Memos licked his parched lips.

"Tap, tap, tap" the happy fuchsia ball started bobbing up and down inside me. As though starting afresh and in better spirits, I put on my faded jeans with the wide black belt, the black sweater and the crocodile boots with the pointed toes, I rinsed and then combed back my curly hair and saw my eyes glowing like coals in the bathroom mirror. "Tap, tap, tap" the happy ball kept bobbing up and down inside me as I walked up Traleon with Memos beside me.

Chapter 13

It was way past midnight when Takis Mararas kicked us out of the Blue Sky. He said he would break both my legs if I ever dared come into his shop again. He didn't want to either see me or hear me. It wasn't bad enough that I had screwed up the neighbour-hood he grew up in, he said, I had the audacity to make trouble in his shop in the company of the weasel (that's what he called Memos) and chase the customers away. Customers, my ass; some schoolboys and a couple of old bikers with earrings, silver chains around their waists, stretched tattoos on their hands and backs and black leather pants that barely buttoned, with their Harleys parked outside like hearses and two faded blondes in their fifties gripping the cue stick the way Rita Hayworth gripped the long black pipe in *Casablanca*, I think.

Things got heated when, after a dozen beers or so, Memos said as a joke to one of the old biker gals that the felt was not insured and I laughed my head off. What he lacked in height, he made up for in wit, if he wanted to. Without thinking twice, the sixty-year-old with the tinted pompous hair and the all-white moustache seized Memos by the collar and told him right to his face that anyone who bothered his little lady might as well have signed his death penalty. Then I gently placed my cue stick on the felt and came from the opposite side of the table and sat next to Memos. I turned to face the chap and with squinty eyes I asked him whether his toothless old trout behind me was his little lady. He turned red as a beetroot and tried to punch me in the face, but I was quick to duck down and his hand landed on the gal's face. The felt reddened.

That's when Takis threw us out. I told him it wasn't right to turn away old customers. Mararas told me to drop the act, and that he couldn't care less about that nickel and dime we gave him once in a blue moon. The door to Blue Sky shut behind us making the same noise as when his father's coffin was shut two years later on the pavement opposite my house. I left like a wet cat. I couldn't afford to act tough around Takis, who was over six feet tall and familiar and totally streetwise. I avoided him ever since I was a kid, just like kittens avoid the tomcat, and the times that I did happen to go against him have been etched on my memory.

"How about we get some *tsipouro* at Epirotiko?" Memos suggested.

"Why not! We've got nothing to lose!" I said and kicked a can of beer down the pavement.

We were heading up Traleon when just before its intersection with Foka I felt the pinball inside me waking up again and its colourful balls pounding me "tap, tap, tap." I turned around.

"Where are you going, you prick? This is the way." Memos was confused. But I picked up the pace without replying. He followed me closely and caught up with me just before the square. "Hey man, where are you going?" he nudged me.

"To Sotiria." I pointed to the flashing lamppost in the corner of Saint Andreas.

"Fine. Then I'm headed home too," he said, and walked down the road spitting, coughing and singing, sometimes loudly, sometimes softly *"Oh, Annoula of the snow."*

The bell of Saint Andreas tolled once. "Tap, tap, tap" the shiny ball jolted my insides. I turned left onto Labrinis and walked past the square thinking how I was making zig-zags on the black asphalt. The block of flats at the corner was pitch black. I eagerly climbed the three steps to the entrance and rung the bitch's doorbell. Shortly after, Sotiria's torpid voice asked over the intercom who it is.

"It's me Stratos, let me in Sotiria my love," I said with a sob and she let me in. Somewhat foggy, I climbed the stairs two at a time and knocked gently on her door.

"Let me in, let me in, I can't take it anymore..." I hummed.

I waited and I waited, but no response. Why is she taking so long, I think to myself, and I knock again. Not a soul! I wait a little longer and then I press my finger on the doorbell whose shrill sound cuts through the night, until the manager comes out in his pyjamas.

"Who are you looking for at this hour, son?" he looks at me through the thick lenses of his glasses, trying to hold back a yawn.

"My Sotiria, sir," I said and the joyful "tap, tap" inside me drained like water in a bathtub when the plug is pulled.

"Sotiria's mum lives on the floor below and you, my child, are bladdered," he said and I teared up.

He took me by the hand and we walked down to the second floor. We knocked. We could hear a commotion inside. I knocked again. Nothing.

"Sotiria, open the door, Sotiria my love, open it, why won't you let me in?"

"I can't. My mother has the key," my wife's voice sounded thin.

"Are you crying, Sotiria honey? Are you crying? Katina, let me in or I'll break your bones one by one, for keeping my wifey locked up." I started kicking and banging on the door. The manager fled right then and there.

I felt weak at the knees and I sat on the steps like a beaten dog. Inside, people shouted and pushed. It made my blood boil and I knocked again. "Sotiria dear, Nickie, let me in." I heard the security chain move and the door opened half-way. Through the crack, I saw the old woman's face.

"Get out of here, you bloody toerag. Get out of here, you lunatic!" her voice echoed through the corridor.

"You're the lunatic Katina, you and your whole clan for not letting me see my family. Sotiria, come out now."

Sotiria begged the old bag to step away from the door, but she was being as stubborn as a mule. She was probably afraid that if she opened the door, all hell would break loose.

"Get out of here, you penniless piece of shit or I'll call 999," squeaked Katina.

"You can call 999, or even 1000, I'm not afraid of anyone. So now, I'm penniless, eh? All the times when I came by bringing you goodies, you opened the door wide for me and called me your son."

"I never wanted you for my son-in-law."

"Is that so, you stupid tart? So, Sotiria was unlucky enough to get mixed up with the likes of me? Wait until I get my hands on you, you won't get rid of me that easily," I said and after giving the door a good kick, I headed downstairs, and ripped out the water bottles and the Ficus that the lunatic had hung all around the hallway and the stairwell, supposedly as decor.

Cursing, singing and breaking the pots in front of me, I made my way to the pavement across the street. I pulled out my mobile phone and called Sotiria. Nothing. It was four o'clock when I started shouting:

"Sotiria, Sotiria... Katina, fuck off, you cunt!"

Then the shutter opened and the old woman started hurling whatever piece of glass she could find, trying to hit me on the head so that the world would be spared from the monster, so she explained frantically. The street was covered with glass and blood. Sotiria was yelling "help!" and her mother was having a nervous breakdown.

"My heart!" shouted Katina on the balcony. "My heart!" and other such stuff, the way the actress Rena Vlahopoulou did in Cry Wolf.

Before long the police showed up and arrested me.

Chapter 14

"Well, well. If it isn't the guys!" I said, recognizing the copper who was smoking and biting his nails the previous day at the police station. They took me to the same old office and dumped me in the same chair across from the same officer. He rolled his eyes and was about to note down the incident in his book, when the door opened and, like the sun, Sotiria entered in the company of my aunt Helen.

"Good morning, Officer," Sotiria said.

"Good morning. Who are you and what do you want?" he asked, vexed.

"I'm Stratos' wife and I've come to pick him up."

"Pick him up to take him where?" he scanned her from head to foot, as if she had descended from Mars.

"Home, Officer." Sotiria looked him straight in the eye.

Hats off to you, Sotiria, for being one tough cookie and cleaning up after me, I pondered proudly.

"As stipulated by the law, Stratos was caught in flagrante delicto for disturbing the peace, and will get the corresponding sentence. If you have the money, you'll get him out; otherwise, he will holiday in Korydallos prison for a month or so," the officer stopped her in her tracks.

"As far as I know, Officer, no one has filed a complaint against him." Sotiria didn't fall for it.

"Look here madam, don't tell me how to do my job. Your husband is being prosecuted ex officio for disturbing the peace," said the copper.

"Stratos didn't hurt anybody, Officer. If he's hurting someone with his drinking, it's himself," said Sotiria almost in tears.

"Within the last month he has troubled us at least three times with his quarrels and brawls with the neighbours and, to make matters worse, on Tuesday he disrupted the Counter Terrorism agency together with his mate, Memos Papadogiorgas–another nice guy," the pig snorted.

"They were drunk, Officer, and when they drink, they fight to the finish. I swear on my child that when he's in his right mind, he's incapable of hurting anybody."

"But he did know how to snitch!" he snapped.

"It was the booze talking, Officer, not my Stratos. Please, hand him over to me and I promise you he will never trouble the agency again," resumed Sotiria.

"Do you hear what your wife says, Achtidis? If you promise me we won't be seeing you again soon, I won't log tonight's incident in the book," the officer softened.

"On my military honour, Officer," I responded.

"On what?" He blushed like an angry turkey.

"Officer, I served as a staff sergeant in the Hellenic Commando Unit," I responded.

"And how come you ended up like this? I don't want to ever see you in that terrible shape again."

"Yes, Officer."

I gave him a military salute and walked out with my arms around Sotiria and the "tap, tap" ahead of us, rolling down the stairs of the police station. My aunt left us somewhere near home, where we arrived at dawn. I followed Sotiria as if in a dream. I was cold. The morning twilight pierced my ribs and my teeth were chattering.

"Are you cold?" she asked with fatigue stamped on her face.

"No, Sotiria dear," I said and felt grateful for her and ashamed of myself for tormenting a woman like that.

At the entrance of our block of flats, we heard Dessie's dog barking as if it had smoked a carton of cigarettes. Stepping out of the lift on the third floor, we run into the smell of Ajax for floors that poured out in the corridor, given that when me and Memos went out that afternoon, I had left the door wide open.

"How did you get like this, Stratos, my darling? You couldn't even close our door?" said Sotiria crying.

I didn't speak. I felt my legs shaking and I staggered, but she was quick to prop me up. She dragged me to the bed and made me lie down. The digital clock on my bedside table read six twenty. My strength had run out. I squeezed my eyes shut. Soon I felt the bed creak and Sotiria's warm body next to me. I buried my face in her heavy boobs and sank into a safe and luminous world.

Chapter 15

I woke to the voice of my mother, chatting with Sotiria and smoking, like always, on the front balcony. It was well after dark. With my ribs piercing through my skin, I crawled towards the lounge in the dim light and after a while I managed to approach them, staggering.

"How are you, son?" my mother asked me with a broken voice and a face like a drizzled pavement.

I sat next to Sotiria and lit one of her cigarettes.

"How do you think, mother? As you know, the day before yesterday I played a joke on Memos with the Counter Terrorism agency, to pass the time. Sotiria flew off the handle and went to her mother's. I waited a whole day for her to come back and when I realized she wasn't coming, I went and brought her back. You gave birth to me, and you know the kind of person I am and how the recession is to blame for all this. Because if I had a job, I wouldn't be drinking and if I didn't drink, all this mess wouldn't have come about. For five whole months I begged Taratselis to give me twenty days' wages and once they were up, I was out of work again. I haven't had a regular job in over a year and who knows whether I'll get to work again like a human being. Booze was my only consolation. I drank to forget and not to feel ashamed, and the more I drank, the more my situation took a turn for the worse."

"Be patient, son, and God will provide."

"God will provide, mother, I won't."

"What is mine is yours. You also have the rent from the shop. Your wife is a good housewife and a hard worker. Quit drinking and be patient. Make sure you're okay and business will pick up," she said and a tear fled her eyes, which narrowed like black buttonholes.

"Go mother, go now. Go home and don't fret. I'll stop drinking and I won't make any more trouble. No more crazy stuff, I swear to you. Leave, mother. I want to be alone with my wife."

Chapter 16

For a whole week I paced back and forth like a beast, from the lounge to the balcony and from the balcony to the lounge, smoking like a chimney. It's a good thing that Sotiria is a chain smoker and she didn't make me quit smoking on top of the booze. Friday at the crack of dawn there is shouting and a ruckus coming from heavy machinery down in the street. I go out and what do I see! Stathogiannis' JCB and a three-axle MAN truck in front of Mararas' hut, across the street.

The shop with the huge tin sign PETROGAZ and the large display windows was located on that street, and behind it was a house; two bedrooms all in all. In the one lived Mararas and in the other the Albanian woman who had ruined my party a few days earlier with her pots and pans. In the evenings just about everyone would drop by, from niggers to Chinese, fighting and shouting in foreign languages; turning Mararas' place into the Tower of Babel.

I put my tracksuit on and went down. Stathogiannis was chatting with Palamidis, a contractor I knew, who told me he had acquired Mararas' place in exchange for a flat in the three-storey block of flats he was going to build. By the end of the day, he planned to tear down the shack and clear the lot. Two workers came and went to the room in the back, loading the Albanian woman's belongings into a van, as she squealed like a pig being slaughtered, all the while trying to pry her things out of their hands. When they finished, they forced her and her husband into the van. She hurled curses in Albanian and her husband sang–he was definitely drunk–and you could hear their voices until they turned onto the avenue.

When everything quieted down, Stathogiannis got in his JCB and after crumpling the tin sign, he buried the bottles and the clothesline wire on the terrace, the Albanian's runny nose and the arguments of the new clan under collapsed walls. I took off my jacket and made my way into the dust and rubble, for an Albanian day's wage without the pension stamp, yet I was in my hour of need so I didn't play hard to get with the contractor (a total prick and a skinflint). In the following months we erected the storeys one by one, until from my balcony I could no longer see Petroupolis' quarries and the spotlights of Terra Petra café, that scanned the dark sky and kept me company in that last cigarette. I worked in the mud and the dust, I went home, bathed, and rested while watching TV. On Saturday nights, I would head up to my mother's place, and she would draw a cross on my chest to protect me from the evil eye, and then head up to Saint Andreas for souvlaki and Coca-Cola.

A fine year... It's good to be working, to have money and make your family proud of your success, even your mother-in-law; despite the fact that she goes by the name Katina, that her breath smells of garlic from afar, that in her lower jaw is a mole with black trembling hair, and despite the fact that we were still at each other's throats at the time. At the end of another year, I finished Palamidis' roof and was paid handsomely. In the meantime, I forgot even the smell of alcohol. That year Sotiria conceived our Nikolakis.

"Nickie if it's a girl, Nikos if it's a boy?" my best man asked me when I told him the name before the christening.

"That's how Stratos names his children," I replied and Sotiria, seeing her wallet bulging, the loan taken care of and her car's petrol tank full, didn't make a peep. I had become the man of the house again, her lord and master.

Chapter 17

On November 6th, with the construction nearly over, Nikolakis was born, and by the time Easter came and we opened our windows, the wasp nest had well and truly planted roots in the Tower of Babel across the street. Mararas' daughter was on the first floor to the left, old-Mararas was on the second and the captain next to him. The only ones who weren't there were Takis, Marmaras' eldest, and Dessie with the pool hall, given that Palamidis would by no means agree to concede more than a floor and a half in the exchange arrangement. I was relieved about that, because I didn't like to open the window and see Dessie's face from across the street, but not for long, because come July 2007 they found old-Mararas dead as a doornail. It was in the heat of the night that the funeral parlour guys carried him frozen stiff. The coffin was open wide and waiting on the pavement, like a box of pastries.

"Who would have known the old man was that heavy," hissed the gravedigger and tried to push Mararas' right arm, which was pointing to the sky, into the coffin.

"It won't go in. The bloody thing is petrified," he said and gave up.

"Let me try," the other guy pushed him and after securing the dead arm in the coffin's frame like a broomstick, he pressed it down hard. A dry "crack" much like a reed breaking, cut through the night.

"See how business is done? May he rest in peace," the gravedigger closed the lid as he crossed himself and asked for repentance.

I was sick to my stomach. Sotiria was working the night shift and the kids were are at my mother's. I coughed, but couldn't get rid of the lump stuck in my throat. I needed alcohol. I turned the house upside down to find that bottle of raki which my brother Lefteris had brought from Crete and Sotiria had put out of sight. I found it in the attic and gulped it down.

Given that I was out of the habit for so long, the booze did a job on me and landed me in my mother's street and in the park of Saint Antoniou with the wilted trees. I stood next to the dustbin looking at the detached house on the opposite side with the green walls and the wooden shutters, next to my childhood home with Labro's car electronics repair shop on the ground floor and right next to it the pink neon sign of my aunt Helen's hair salon, flickering: "Haircuts, the Beautiful Helen. Manicure – Pedicure."

It was twilight and I couldn't tell whether it was dusk or dawn. I lit a cigarette and from the first puff I felt her fluffy tail rub up against my legs. A black cat! I was disgusted, but I couldn't move and shake her off my feet; I couldn't even speak. After circling me a few times, she moved away and teasingly sharpened her claws on a tree trunk. She then crossed the deserted road and sat under a street light. She stayed there looking at me, licking her shiny fur. It's going to rain, I thought, and felt a sadness when there was nothing to be sad about. I stepped on my cigarette butt and turned back towards Ano Patissia, when I sensed something tickling against the nape of my neck. I shook off my collar and saw a mouse fall onto the dry flowerbed, looking at me with its beady eyes and vanishing into the sewer.

I woke up in my sleep with Sotiria hovering over me in a furious state of mind. I reeked of something along the lines of sweat and piss and was all sticky against the mattress of the baby's crib. I couldn't even remember how I had gotten there, let alone how a burly man of six foot five like myself managed to fit in the child's crib! I rose embarrassed and went to the bathroom. My body ached as if a train had run me over. I went out into the lounge and crawled to the balcony, under my wife's bleary eyes. What could I possibly tell her; how could I explain? I just drew her attention to the people who had come for the funeral in the old man's balcony and the funeral notice at the entrance of Mararas' place across the street. She shrugged her shoulders indifferently and locked herself up in our room. I spent the night on the sofa like a beaten dog.

Chapter 18

The only thing I remember from the days that followed was the great shame I felt for falling off the wagon and the fact that now that saint woman, Sotiria, thought less of me. I didn't deserve her. I could not hold a candle to her. I knew well that old-Mararas was my alibi for going back to my secret longing. There was no way to justify the terror I felt from the crack of his arm, given that when I was a kid, I used to go to the Second Cemetery at midnight on a full moon and on my way back freaked everyone out with the crosses and the bones I stole from the ossuary. The fact that the old man and I got along well and joked around whenever we met on the street or at the coffee house was no excuse either.

Mararas was a quiet man, nothing like his brats, Takis in particular. Me and my mother used to go to his grocery store to change the gas bottle. I carried the old one on my back and would bring it back full on a broken-down cart. I remember the nearly empty shelves of the store with the expired cans and the dusty pasta and, in the back, the yard with the bottles and the grass growing between them, as well as the old lady Marika washing the old man's underpants in an aluminum washbasin. I hadn't seen the old man since 1986 when we moved to the upper floor of my childhood home and got an electric stove, and I never imagined that I would be there at the demolition of his store, the construction of his new house, and his death.

But as luck would have it, in 1999 I got sick and was taken to Laiko General Hospital with a fever of forty-one. Infectious mononucleosis, the doctors said and they quarantined me. On the third day, when I began getting up and sitting at the table, spring came into the ward.

"Oh, hello there," I said to her and Sotiria gave me a look identical to that of Aliki Vougiouklaki in the film Aliki in the Navy, which made me lose my colour again.

"Are you the new guy?" She half-opened her mouth like bitter almond.

"Why? Do you think I'm chopped liver?"

She didn't reply, instead she placed a yellow urinal next to me and uncapped the syringe.

"What's that, girl?"

"What do you think it is? A lollipop? Did you come here for something else?"

"That's why they brought me in, yet I found you, my mermaid," I said and stretched out my right hand on the table. She searched for a vein on my wrist with shaky hands.

"They usually draw blood from here," I showed her the inner side of my elbow.

"I only know how to draw from here," she said and stabbed me with the syringe. I didn't make a peep.

"Your skin is hard. What do you do for a living?" she asked.

"I am a construction worker, dishy, a roofer and a formworker to be exact. And I'm hard all over." I winked at her meaningfully. She blushed up to her ears and rotated the syringe like a bodkin in the vein she hadn't been able to locate. When she realized that, despite the punctures, she was drawing air, she put a band-aid on and started fumbling my left wrist.

"Not so fast, doll," I said to her. "If you don't find a vein here either, you can still try my legs so you can crucify me like Christ.

I will stay put though, because I like to be tortured by a girl as pretty and full of zest like yourself." I felt her mellow.

Every day for a fortnight–that is how long I stayed at the hospital–I waited for her with a rose and my veins at her disposal. I had ravaged the rosebushes of the adjacent Medical School, which was what she had done to my veins. When I got my discharge slip, I looked for her at the charge nurse's office.

"What do you want Sotiria for?" The charge nurse raised her sour face on me.

"I want to thank her for the care and attention," I said. She looked at me from head to toe and told me that Sotiria was at the nurse's station, two doors down and to the right. For the first time in my life my knees felt weak over a chick. I knocked on the door and my darling Sotiria opened it. Dense smoke was coming from inside. Well, nurses also smoke, I reasoned.

"What is it?" she asked me with a half-smile.

"I just got discharged and figured we should not lose touch," I answered with a doubt in my mind.

"If you want it that bad, I'm in," she puffed the smoke to my face.

"Where can I find you?"

"Come to my neighbourhood on Saturday afternoon at seven. At the square of Saint Andreas in Labrini there's a cafeteria...."

I was stunned.

"Why are you looking at me like that? What's the matter?" she asked.

Then I told her that all our lives we've been neighbours and that fate had us meet at the hospital! That was our stroke of luck. One date and we were an item. From May to September, we rented a one-room flat on the terrace of a block of flats in Ano Patiissia, below the train tracks.

"Where are you off to, girl?" nagged Katina, her mother, who had a hard time accepting the fact that her daughter was going to marry a construction man. "Keep your mind on your school and on your job, get to know him better and if you still match after a couple of years, you marry him."

But at the time Sotiria was saying "It's Stratos all the way" and I was in my best shape. Every Friday, I would empty my pockets and the lounge table would turn green from the five-hundred bills. On Saturdays I would wash the little red Fiat, which I had gotten fourth hand from a retired neighbour cop, and we would head to the clubs in the Corniche. I took her everywhere. *Dionysiou, Mazonakis, Karras*. My darling Sotiria had more than her share of dancing, drinking and all-nighters, and I was gloating for showing up with such a babe. In 2000, she finished her internship and Father Porfyrios, her mother's spiritual counselor, had her placed in the "Saint Kikilia" institution for elders suffering with Alzheimer's. Katina was religious–how could she not be? In spitting distance from Saint Andreas church, her blood had been instilled with incense and with "Lord, have mercy." Before long, we got married and moved to the three-bedroom flat off Olofitou street, just opposite Mararas' place.

The year of 2001 was the best year of my life. Sotiria and I in our own home, with new furniture, a stainless steel refrigerator, dishes and pans and the thousand-bit AKAI that my mother gave me on my name day. We would open the windows and I would turn the volume to the max. The walls would squeak. Two lame spinsters who lived in the house down the street complained that we were bothering them, but we didn't give a sod about that. The neighbourhood slept when we slept, and woke up when we woke up. During the first year I saved up for a down payment and in early 2002, with a loan and a mortgage on my childhood home, I bought the house that we were renting and I became an important somebody in the eyes of Sotiria, her mother and society.

Chapter 19

In mid-August and before his forty-day memorial, they threw Mararas' things away. First the iron bed with the fraying mattress and the box spring that squeaked every time the departed switched sides, then the chest of drawers with the engravings and the oxidised mirror who reflected the midday sun on our balcony before they picked it up, and lastly, the old aluminum pots and the rusty flatware. In two nights, all of Mararas' stuff that his children hadn't been able to tear away from him during two house moves, was lined up on the pavement of Olofitou and Ioannou Foka. Old men don't part with their things. Afterwards, they had the Bulgarian woman who worked for Mr. Vangelis, the quadriplegic on Akrothoon, clean up. For three days Tatiana cleaned and washed the old man's house, crying buckets. And how could she not, when every first day of the month when Mararas got his pension, I would catch her sneaking into his home, taking every precaution not to be seen.

"Let the Bulgarian stick to her last, so the saying goes," I would tell the old man the following day and he would laugh under his moustache and say that he was going to kick my arse. No wonder the Bulgarian couldn't let go of the late man's pension!

At the beginning of September, Takis the firstborn, moved into the departed's flat with Dessie and stuffed the balcony with cartons, toys and broken bicycles. In front of the balcony door, they put a plasma TV which was on around the clock, and outside they tied the poodle, which howled for three days and banged its head against the railing.

"Get the dog!" I shouted at them and they told me to mind my own business. That is when I put the AKAI on at full blast. In a jiffy they got the dog and turned off the TV. They may have kicked me out of their Blue Sky, and I may have gotten occasionally slapped around by Takis, who was five years older and a frigging toerag, but I showed them who's running the neighbourhood from day one.

Chapter 20

The summer of 2007 was a rough one and we made it to the autumn by grumbling, bickering and sulking. Daily wages had become less frequent again and Sotiria no longer made eye contact with me. She would come into the house and her eyes would pass over me as if falling into a void. I sensed her contempt and there were many nights when I would take the boy, who was almost a year old, and go to sleep at my mother's, so that we wouldn't get in her way and irritate her more. My days went sluggishly by from my home to my mother's and to Paranda, where I would make do with one frappé until noon. It's not as if I had another choice, given that I was unwanted at Blue Sky and at IZO. So, I would arrive at Paranda around ten to have my coffee with dignity and when I was short on money, Koula would say with a grin from ear to ear *it's on the house, after all we were neighbours...* It was a thousand times better to look at Lola's ass, than to look at Dessie's fat head with that bleached hair, and those wide hips.

September was on its way out and I still hadn't gotten a day's wage. On the street there was no talk about a new license. Not a wall was built, not a leaf rustled. Until one morning at the Antisteon coffee house I bumped into Taratselis who offered me a roof repair up north. He said that on Tuesday morning at six o'clock, Samras would come and pick me up in his truck, together with Stathogiannis. Eight hundred euros for four days, no pension stamp.

In early October and after ten days of rain, there was a break in the weather. Up north it had rained more and the new roof of the wealthy man leaked. Boo freaking hoo, he should have found a capable handyman before he started. Instead, as he was used to the ease, he had assigned the contractor's work to one of the tacky technical offices that pop up in the north suburbs like mushrooms and instead of handymen they send out Albanians, who are like jacks-of-all-trades. Construction forgives the crooked structure and the careless plasterwork, and many other things, but not the plumbing and the roof. Pipes break if they are not properly soldered together and the roof leaks if it has not been built by a roofer with guts. When the first rains come, things become complicated and then the rich men discover the contractors of the southern suburbs for the odd jobs, yet the big money has been spent elsewhere.

Monday night and in view of work I went to bed early, but the baby who had gotten used to sleeping after one o'clock, rebelled and raised hell as usual. But I did have to wake up early. At twelve o'clock he asked for food. Though he wasn't even one yet, he ate everything. He would eat us if he could. As soon as he quieted down, I switched sides, but the minute I fell asleep he started hitting his empty plate with the spoon. I got up angry and went into the lounge ready to let him have it.

"Will you be quiet, you little shit, or am I going to throw you off the balcony?"

The kid shoved his head under the sofa cushions and pretended to snore.

"Take it easy," Sotiria said, "now, go lie down."

It was a quarter to one. I lay down and as I was thinking about my summers in Antista and my grandmother's pit in Agrilies, and the frogs that paddled sometimes in the pit and other times in the ditch, and the tadpoles that creased the greenish mirror of the water from side to side, when I get slapped in the eye by the moron and I fly off the handle. Without thinking twice, I smack the brat in the chest with such force that he hits the floor like a watermelon, crying. That night the baby slept at two and I had no more than three hours of sleep until six o'clock when Sotiria nudged me, as I heard neither the alarm clock ringing next to me nor Smaras' honking from the street.

I staggered out, feeling like there were a thousand needles poking my dry eyes. The asphalt road was soaked and the icy breeze blowing from the avenue's direction stung my bare arms. Stathogiannis, his curly hair tangled in the rain-laden clouds, waited standing up on the Datsun's truck bed and Smaras was smoking his strong cigarette at the steering wheel. I greeted them both and unlocked my warehouse that faces the street. With Stathogiannis' help I loaded the Black+Decker, the welding equipment and the extension cords, and after tying the scaffold with straps, like I have done a thousand times, I jumped on the trailer, felt a "clack" in my right leg and collapsed on the asphalt with a stabbing pain in my kidneys.

"Are you hurt, wanker?" Stathogiannis landed next to me.

"What's wrong with you, mate?" Smaras rushed to me.

"Come on, stand up slowly."

"I can't, mate," I bit my lip and showed him my right toes that were facing my back. His face turned pale.

"Get Sotiria," I managed to mutter.

I felt a weariness and a sadness rising from my chest and gripping my throat. My eyes narrowed. I woke up in the ambulance with a shooting pain in my waist and foot. We made it to KAT and, before long, I ended up in a small room in the company of an intern and a nurse.

"It could have been a fracture; you got off easy. You seem like a tough cookie," said the doctor and tossed me a pillow.

"Man, it hurts a lot, but it lasts seconds. Bite this."

The nurse grabbed my calf with claw-like hands, a burly guy six foot tall, and the doctor flipped my leg. I was scared shitless, but didn't make a peep. Stratos is not a sissy to start crying. Then, they put me in a cast for a month–goodbye, wages–, they did a second set of x-rays and sent me to get an abdominal ultrasound, seeing that I felt as if a steamroller had run over my kidneys.

We arrived at Evangelismos hospital by twelve and before a doctor could check me out the pain was gone.

"Let's get out of here," I told Sotiria.

"No. Since we've come this far, we'll wait," she said angrily.

The pathologist checked me at three (if there was something seriously wrong with me, I would have kicked the bucket by then) and said that I needed an ultrasound–old news that one. From three to four I drank five glasses of water and waited in the wheelchair for my turn to come. That is when Taratselis arrived, with Jenny, that blonde halfwit with the open mouth he had recently picked up from the Association of Antisteon, of which he was president.

"Nephew, what's the matter?" he asked gloomily."

"I missed out on the daily wages, old chap," I said, all bitter.

"Make sure you get well and we'll find some more. How are you, now?"

"How should I be? I've had five glasses of water and still not ready to piss."

"Hey, that's how these things are. You have to be patient with the hydraulics," he said and whispered something in Jenny's ear. They both laughed.

"What did he say that made you laugh, you stupid bitch?" I turned and said to the halfwit. She thought I was paying her a compliment and started cackling.

"Quiet!" the charge nurse poked her head out from the plexiglass shack in the corridor.

"Get her out of here because I'll shred her to pieces," I said to Sotiria pointing at Jenny.

They took me for my ultrasound at four thirty. There was a young lady doctor with long blonde hair. I wanted to piss so much I could burst. Sotiria helped me up on the bed.

"Now, get out please, I don't need you anymore," said the doctor to my wife.

"But, I'm a nurse."

"It's fine, go out and we won't be long," she said sternly and turned off the light. She spread that disgusting gel on my belly and started looking around dictating the readings to the girl sitting at the computer.

"Careful, or there may be complications," I told her when her thingy reached down low in my belly. She didn't say a thing; she didn't even smile. These lady doctors are completely uptight, no sense of humour.

When the exam was over, they called for Sotiria, who pushed me into a toilet on the opposite side, where a person could hardly fit and the shit was up to the ceiling.

"I can't," I told her, "I'd rather pee myself."

She called me a difficult patient and brought me a bedpan. In a corner of the hallway, crowded by patients and relatives, I peed. That's national health system for you.

With the ultrasound results we went back to the pathologist again, who said he saw something in the left kidney which may have existed before the fall. In order to make sure it wasn't pathological, he was going to keep me until noon the next day, by then he would have my 24-hour-exams, and provided there was no change, he would discharge me. I was pissed off. No, I wasn't going to stay, I told Sotiria, who told me to cut out that macho stuff and do as the doctor instructed. Then she rushed to see to my admission and left me in the outpatient clinic with Taratselis and the bimbo who wanted to sign my cast no matter what.

"How can you sign it? When you don't even know how to write," I cut her off.

The leg was bothering me and my eyes were heavy, when my mother showed up with my aunt Helen, who saw Taratselis and Jenny and blew a fuse.

"What's she doing here?" she asked furiously.

"What do you mean? She is the secretary of the Association of Antisteon. She is here to see Stratos who is a founding member," he said apathetically.

"You better take her and get out of here before I pluck every single hair out of her head!" my aunt started shouting.

"Shut up, Helen," my mother took her aside in despair.

Everyone had turned and was looking at us. Feeling embarrassed, Taratselis got Jenny and vanished into thin air. We went up to Pathology Section B, I took the lift because of the wheelchair and she took the stairs. Into my aunt's cheeks two thick black lines were carved.

"Wipe your tears and stop dumping your boyfriend troubles on us. As if my being a mess is not bad enough, I have you acting like an eighteen-year-old over Taratselis. He's not even decent looking," I said to her, all wound up.

Helen went downstairs to cry in peace. The stretcher-bearer took my papers to the charge nurse and came back to take me to my bed, located in the clinic's corridor! I went ballistic.

"For twenty years I've been collecting pension stamps for heavy-duty jobs to get thrown in the corridor? Fuck your bloody ESY!" I said to the nurse who came to make the camp bed.

"Take your complaints to the ministry," she replied and, without paying any attention to me, continued making my bed. With my blood boiling, I took the pyjamas my mother had brought and pulled down my trousers.

"What are you doing, there?" the charge nurse rushed over red in the face.

"I'm putting my pyjamas on and, before you come in, please knock on my room door," I said to her and, ignoring the doctors, the nurses and the patients passing by, I changed my clothes.

I lay down and as I hadn't slept at all the night before, I fell fast asleep. From what Sotiria told me later, no one in the corridor could get a moment's peace with my snoring. Even the professor who came by dragging behind him a bunch of young doctors, stopped to ask her:

"Is that how he snores?"

"He could do worse," Sotiria replied.

At about six o'clock, Sotiria took my mother and my aunt and left for a while. Around eight, while I was soundly sleeping, they came and took me to a room that had been vacated in the meantime. I was dumbfounded when I went in. They had given me a single room, with a flower pot on the table and a desk in the corner! The perks of anyone who snores!

"How am I to spend the whole night in here by myself? I get the creeps," I told the nurse, who went out hastily, only to return momentarily with the charge nurse to draw my blood.

"Girls, why don't you keep me company?" I asked them and they disappeared in a flash. Apparently, they were scared of me. I don't mind, I love nurses, which is why I married one of them.

Chapter 21

On Wednesday noon we returned home, where my mother was waiting for us with the children and Anna. Mrs. Nickie came over and hugged me and the baby started crying as soon as he saw me with the bandaged leg and the crutches.

"See what happens when you don't let me sleep, you prick?" I asked him.

"Stop guilt-tripping the child," Sotiria said.

"Guilt, my ass. Nobody ever cared about my guilt," I muttered, and then fell asleep, after telling the baby that if he continued to make so much noise, I would strangle him like a chicken.

I woke up after seven still feeling fatigued, and with a heavy heart and empty pockets. Sotiria was cooking and mumbling behind the counter. She was saying "You're careless. You don't look where you step, you just run around like a young bear." I understood the part about the bear and I asked her if she was talking about herself, with that fat face.

"Did you call me fat, Strato darling?" she glared at me and I felt the urge to hit her in the head with the ashtray full of cigarette butts or beat her with the crutches, but I restrained myself and I shut up, primarily because I needed her, and secondly, because unless she did something terribly wrong to me–which she actually did–I'd be the last man on earth to raise a hand to his wife after that incident in the village many years ago:

That morning my father returned home bladdered and my mother was not there to get him something to drink. He looked in every nook and cranny for *tsipouro* and not being able to find one, he broke our last shot glasses out of spite and then waited for her so he could give her a piece of his mind. The moment he saw her taking her shoes off out of the door and coming inside exhausted with the milk churn, he asked her:

"Where have you been, you cow?"

"With the animals, where else!" Where have you been all night long?" she replied, setting the churn in front of the sink.

"Tell me who you've been running around with, you cunt!" his eyes turned black with rage and came up to her as she sat on the divan by the corner.

"You have no right to call me a cunt when you've been drunk every day since you came back from Athens," shouted Mrs. Nickie and leaned forward to toss two logs into the fire. Without saying a word, he grabbed her by her braid, and started kicking her every which way. My mother, cramped between the fireplace and the divan, took his blows, unable to get away. I rushed in to deliver her from his hands, without minding getting in the line of fire.

My father told me to get the hell out of there and he kept kicking. Seeing that I was getting nowhere, I climbed up on the divan and pulled his hair. In his drunken stupor, he gave me a big slap that pinned me flat against the smudged wall while he continued punching my mother. I came out of the house screaming "Help! Help! My mother..." feeling my voice getting caught in the freezing fog.

"Panayio, Panayio!" I banged on my neighbour's door, which she opened with flour on her hands. The fresh dough rested on the table and the roaster was burning peacefully in the fireplace. "Panayio," I said breathlessly, "he's killing her."

She didn't ask me who; the whole village knew that my father would get drunk and beat up my mother. The neighbour hung her apron on the doorknob and came out shaking the flour off her hands. We headed for the house, which shimmered in the fog. The plane leaves creaked under our feet. The house was silent. Panayio pushed open the door.

"Nick, Nick, where are you?"

"I'm here, Panayio, where else? Here, with the cunt," his voice was tangled in his smoker's cough.

I sat on the ledge with the same anxiety as that time I was waiting side by side with my father for my mother to give birth to Leonidas. From the back of the house came Panayio's scream:

"You beast, you crippled her."

I became dizzy and fell on the cold paving stones of the courtyard, from where grandfather Leonidas lifted me when he arrived with grandmother and two neighbours, after being notified by Panayio's son. I squeezed myself on the ledge. No one bothered with me any longer. I heard grandmother's screams and curses for that good-for-nothing man who had crippled my mother.

"There's no one's fault but my own. I'm the one who gave my girl to the drunkard's son, the killer's grandson and I might as well have buried her with my own two hands. I swear on my dying breath that if she pulls through, you'll never get to lay eyes on her, you bastard."

The two neighbours went out and soon returned with a stretcher.

"What's the matter with my mother?" I asked one of them, the one I felt bold enough with.

"He roughed her up. We are taking her to the hospital."

I felt myself trembling. From inside, you could hear grandmother's crying and other people's voices, as they were trying to get mother on the stretcher. After a long while, the panels of the green front door opened like the beautiful gate and let her out.

"Mum!" I rushed to her. "Mum..."

She half-opened her eyes which were bruised and badly swollen, and whispered something through her lips that were blown up like glimmering bloody bubble gum.

"What did you say, mum?" I shouted and stood on tiptoe in order to reach her and hug her, without success.

"Don't be afraid, Stratos my love, I'm fine. Take care of Left..." her phrase was left hanging in mid-air by a grimace suggesting considerable pain.

I let her go and as she was being lifted, her left calf hung from the stretcher with the hands of our metal clock imprinted on it. Ten minutes past eleven, I recognized the time, painfully. I stayed behind watching them carry her on their backs towards Saint George. They would take her, they said, up to the plane trees on the public road, where there was going to be a car passing by that would drive her into town.

Grandmother took me into her house. Lefteris was there. The kid had no idea, his head had always been in the clouds. Grandmother made pancakes. I ate one and my eyes fell on the alarm clock on top of the fireplace. It was two o'clock. I remember the time on my mother's naked calf and started crying.

"Oh, come on, shame on you!" grandfather said. "You're a grown man and you're acting like a toddler. Soon you'll be off to the army, fighting for your country."

I didn't respond, I just went out on the pretext I was going outside to wash up in the tap. But instead, I walked up to my house. With a wild thumping kicking my chest, I turned left to the foot of our plot and through the fog which had by now thinned out, I saw the policeman entering our house dragging behind him a rough, black wooden thing, similar to my mother's rolling pin, but much longer and thicker. I hid in the Cyclop's cave–that's how we used to call the rock in the middle of our plot–and waited for the cop to come out and see him head uphill.

When his green uniform disappeared behind the trunks of the bare plane trees climbing the mountain top, I ran home. I entered with a shudder. The fire was burning. On the concrete in front of the corner and on the foot of the fireplace my mother's blood was drying. A sour smell mixed with freshly-burned wood was in the air. The divan bedding was ruffled and the chairs were turned upside down. Father was nowhere to be seen. I sat at the edge of the divan and looked around me without knowing what to think or do, when I heard a moan from the bedroom. I approached on tiptoes and peeked in through the half-open door. My father with his head buried in the red wool shag rug was panting. "Oh, oh, dear God." I hurriedly went to him and hugged his cloaked head, crying.

It was November and mother came home on Christmas Eve. My father wouldn't raise his eyes to her and I searched under her sock for the hands of the clock. Mother cooked the meat that grandfather Leonidas and grandmother had brought her; pleading with her to leave us and return to her childhood home. But she looked them in the eye and, stroking Lefteris' head who clung to her skirt, told them that she had made the decision to stay with her husband and children.

We sat at the table, crossed ourselves and started eating silently. We couldn't eat a thing. Father dropped his fork and started crying. We run to hug him. He kneeled down before my mother and started rolling down the sock on her left foot. When he came across the scar of the clock, he leaned forward to kiss it. My mother's tears fell like rain upon him and upon us. That night, father swore that before the start of the new year, he would take us with him to Athens, where Taratselis had a job for him, that he would finish the house on the plot in Patissia, which was my mother's dowry, that he would make her the lady of the house, like she deserved, that he would quit drinking and that he would never raise a hand to her again. He'd rather have his hand cut off.

And that's what happened, except for the alcohol, which he kept on consuming, until it consumed him.

Chapter 22

Apart from the afternoons when my mates took me out, I spent an entire month going from my bedroom to the lounge and from the lounge to the balcony. I smoked ten Marlboro cartons. Sotiria had a long face and the boy kicked my casted leg.

"Wait until I get well, you son of a gun and I'll show you," I would tell him and he would burst out laughing. The kid is a copy of me, brilliant, a star; that little bastard is the spitting image of me.

The confinement had made me edgy and restless.

"Drop me off at the square for an hour or so to have a cup of coffee and meet people," I implored Sotiria and she would get furious.

"I work day and night, I cook, I wash, I iron, I take care of the children, I don't have time to pee, and you want me to give you a ride?" she would retort.

That prick Memos didn't show up either. He was busy with work, said Annoula one day, when she came upstairs to ask to borrow coffee. I told her to cut the crap, but I restrained myself because my relationship with Sotiria would go tits up, given that she had made it quite clear that I was in no way to bring my cockfighting into our home–that's how she referred to my dispute with Memos. Anna was her best friend, her person, and she wouldn't allow me to ruin their friendship. So, I shut my mouth and bought this lie. Memos at work seems like a joke.

Thank God for Stathogiannis and Smaras who from day two and at least three times a week, would take me up to the square for coffee and chat, and then managed to carry me to the local *ouzerie* for nibbles. Twice they took me to the Avenue Stadium to gate thirty-three, to blow off some steam. It didn't pan out so well, however, because the score was 0-1 the first time, and 1-3 the second. The team was going from bad to worse at that time. "The way I see it, we'll be in the non-professional league," I said and Smaras would get depressed, while Stathogiannis and I would laugh out loud. And in addition to the rides, when they returned me home late at night, they even gave me some pocket money! "Take this for cigarettes," they would shove the money in my pocket and I would get all teared up. Better than brothers.

Anyway, when it comes to brothers I had failed miserably. Unfortunately, you do not get to choose your relatives, you just get them. That's how I got Lefteris, or rather Lefteris got me. He was born grumpy and down on his luck, lazy and greedy, he clung to me like a barnacle, probably my mother sewed him on me like a button that couldn't be unstitched. "Take your brother with you," she would push him on me when I went to the vacant lot for some rock fighting or to the neighbourhood uphill for climbing. I never enjoyed a carefree game as a kid. My mind was always on the sickly brat who would start crying at the drop of a hat and would rat me out to Mrs. Nickie, who always believed him and punished me for things that weren't my fault. Because I pushed him or told him to go home alone or because I kicked him during football and all that other stuff that happens during playtime. My only good moments with him were when I played the Karagiozis show in the village and he passed me the figures in order, and although he couldn't read yet, he did the Kolitiri very successfully. Until the night he put the lamp too close to the curtain covering the window of grandfather Stratos' old house, where the performances took place, and the cloth and the figures caught fire and my career as a Karagiozis-puppeteer came to an inglorious end.

"Time to call it a night," bristled grandfather Stratos who chased us away.

Growing up, Lefteris was still the person he was as a boy. He barely finished an electricians' school and my mother set him up with a company that assembled Legrand panels. There he got involved with the boss's daughter, a big brunette girl, named Kathraki. Even now I still can't tell what she saw in him. Apparently, there was more to Lefteris than meets the eye. At twenty-three he married Kathraki and moved to her penthouse in Kypseli, where he lived the good life for ten years and would still be living there, had he not gotten mixed up with the Albanian woman who was the company's cleaning lady. The Achtidis clan are shaggers all right. So, one Easter the phone rang at dawn: it was Mrs. Nickie telling me we should go and pick him up, but that's another story, which may be suited for later.

Anyway, that month was a rough one. Deep inside, however, I believed that everything was going to change for the better, until one day I actually heard on the TV, which played at full blast from morning to night and kept me company, about the EEC subsidies to new businesses for young, unemployed people and the idea of the Tsunami struck me. An amazing, no-cost idea. I was going to tell Labro to move his electronics repair shop out of the ground floor of my childhood home on Saint Antoniou, and with the subsidy I would open an elite car wash and polish business! Come summer I would be somewhat better off and I would finally take Sotiria to Paros, where she had been dying to go all those years. There wasn't a single nurse who didn't want to go to Paros. So much for the island. In a year or so I would trade her Fiat for a shiny red Toyota convertible and finally get to see her smiling at me like she used to. I would be the man of the house again, like the time when I emptied my pockets and the coffee table in the lounge turned green.

Chapter 23

At the time that the idea of the Tsunami came to me, I had just had my cast removed and immediately after that a construction site in Varympompi turned up. One evening around seven o'clock my cell phone rang. Sotiria was sleeping in the other room and the kid was watching cartoons. I didn't feel like picking up, but it kept ringing so I answered it. It was Taratselis.

"My dear nephew, we have just signed a four-storey construction job in Varympompi. You're in charge of formwork and the roof. We start Monday morning. Are you in?"

I jumped up like the spring and limped around the lounge tripping over the furniture.

"What's gotten into you – you're acting childish?" asked Sotiria who had in the meantime woken up by the commotion and was headed my way like a boat in a storm.

"I got a job!" I shouted and threw the kid into the air, who burst out laughing.

"Pour us a whisky to celebrate," I said to her and she brought out the Jack Daniels without further ado.

The boy was throwing blocks at my head and I was talking to her about jobs; plural. I had the feeling that I was stuck under the frozen surface of a lake in Greenland and just as I was about to let the salty water permeate my lungs, I was met with good fortune, and with a hammer that punched the life-saving hole. I rose to the surface and started taking deep breaths. I knew that luck wouldn't abandon me. Life was once again sweet and welcoming.

Chapter 24

Saturday afternoon, mid-November and after the first week in Varympompi, I went down to my mother's to talk to her about the shop.

"Mother, I want to talk to you about a business I'm thinking of setting up which won't leave me high and dry again."

Mrs. Nickie wiped her wet hands on her flowered apron with the big blue pockets and sat down across from me. She took a cigarette and lit it and I began to narrate her the story about the Tsunami. After listening to me carefully, she said:

"What does the best roofer of Athens have to do with suds and lubricants? You better concentrate on your work, you hear me! Labros is a good handyman and for twenty-one years he hasn't been a day late with his rent. As long as he's working, you have your monthly income come rain or shine, whether you work or not. You don't have to worry about how you're going to pay your house loan."

"Mother, the Olympics have used up the concrete and the bricks from the Attica basin and have done away with construction for the next hundred years. And besides, I'm getting older. I've been on the scaffold since I was eighteen. For twenty whole years I've been slaving with formwork and roofs. It's time I change professions. I can't keep begging Taratselis and every other stupid contractor for daily wages. I have a family and responsibilities. I must have a permanent job and security. As for the loose change Labros gives me, when I open the shop, I will be able to make that in half a day."

I tried this and I tried that, and after a couple of cigarettes Mrs. Nickie caved. What blind man doesn't want to see; what mother doesn't want what's best for her child? She promised me that she would go down to see Labros and tell him to vacate as soon as possible.

On my way out, I passed by Paranda.

"One sweet frappé with milk, and don't forget, Lola, three spoonfuls of sugar," I said to the chick, who didn't seem to understand that I was drooling over her.

Part
three

Chapter 25

Labros and his wife were on their knees, pleading with me. To show patience. To give them more time until they find another place. As if it was easy to find a place to set up an electrics repair shop in an area that was riddled with auto repair shops, body shops, marble shops, and flower shops. Right from the start I made it clear to them that I was in a hurry. How could I wait until August 2008, as they asked me to, when the subsidies for starting a new business were due to expire in March? I had responsibilities that couldn't wait, I was raising two kids. Kalliopi did everything in her power to convince me. The woman who patted my head with the golden rods jingling on her wrist and a bunch of golden rings when she came upstairs with the red wallet under her armpit to pay the rent and lay out in front of my mother the dresses and the amulets, the scarfs, the slippers and the boots, the jackets and the skirt-suits, the coats and the two-pieces that Labros had bought her, was now on her knees, begging me. But I wouldn't budge. I wanted to have my shop and I wanted it yesterday. They had been taking advantage of it long enough. It was time for someone else besides them to make a living out of it. I cut her off. After all, I could kick them out whenever I wanted. We hadn't signed a contract since 2000.

At the end of December, they found a shack upstreet on Orfanidou and got the hell out. The moment they did, I took Mrs.

Nickie and a hose and we wiped the shop clean; it hadn't met with a broom and a dustpan since we rented it to them.

"How could Kalliopi find the time to clean up? She was too busy with hairdressers, makeovers and bikini lasers," my mother growled through clenched teeth, pointing to the dirt and stench.

That day we had the baby with us. Sotiria happened to work in the morning, Anna, Memos' wife, was in bed with the flu, my aunt next door had one appointment after another and my mother-in-law was in the village for the olive harvest. When times were hard, the old bag would flee. Nickie was at daycare. The baby ate the chocolate my mother gave him and, despite the low temperature, started rolling half-naked in the suds, the grease and the tar until late in the afternoon when his mother came to collect him, completely black and freezing. This kid doesn't worry me, he's hardy, a pure Spartan.

With Smaras' help, within a week I laid the floor and walls up to the ceiling with thirty-by-sixty blue granite tiles. Then we took down the front window glass and Taratselis' aluminium worker installed two electric shutters with Ciza security locks for me. In mid-January 2008, the machines came. An automatic car wash station, two foam sprayers, one bio-cleaning upholstery extractor, one power extractor and two carpet beaters–all German, brand new, with a three-year warranty. Late January, I filed the paperwork for the permit, which would take three months, but I, who needed it in a month's time, bribed two clerks and they brought it to the house ten days later. I was prepared. We live in Greece, after all.

Once everything was set up, I had Smaras hang the Tsunami neon label, which flashed next to my aunt's hair salon sign like a drugstore sign. Meanwhile, Taratselis' construction was progressing. It felt really good that instead of sitting and waiting for the roof as I did in the past, I was now working my ass off at the Tsunami and when the time came, I would head up to Varympompi to grab my eight grand. Everything was falling into place. I had a headache almost daily and I would get my aunt from next door to ward off the evil eye; she showed me how oil became one with water.

"They have their eyes on you. We've landed in the world's worst neighbourhood. Nobody wants to see their fellow men make something of themselves, damn them," Helen would say, drawing a cross on me.

Chapter 26

Saturday, March 1st, 2008 was the day of the opening. I brought the stereo from the house, picked up five cases of beer and wine in bulk from Sklavenitis, set up my mother's grill in the street and had Simos, an old classmate and neighbour who dropped in uninvited, grill skewers and pies. Simos was kind of a moron as a kid, but he was top choice for the grill. *Everyone has a specialty and Loumidis has coffee,* as the advert goes. My mother made Ravani cake and Sotiria brought a big box of millefeuille she had pinched from the nursing home. We played music at full blast. Koula and Lola served wine, beer and refreshments. It was a shindig.

Taratselis was the first one in to bring his ride, which I put in the automatic station. We all stayed and watched the wash with suspense, as if we were in the stadium; and the brushes stroking the car, as if we were watching porn. When I pulled the car out onto the pavement opposite the box, they applauded by raising their glasses to me, and Taratselis stuck a fifty euro note, the easiest to earn in all my life, right between my eyes. "This is for good luck. Congratulations, my nephew," he said and groped my aunt.

At around three o'clock we started dancing in the middle of the street. My mother and my mother-in-law were in the lead, my aunt Helen was behind and Taratselis was next to her, squeezing her hand while she pretended to pull it. She was still sulking because of the hospital, but she was a real glutton for punishment. The voices and songs blended with the "ding, ding, ding" of the bell of Saint Isidoron, which tolled every time someone boarded the train to the other side. Oh well, the dead with the dead and the living with the living.

In the evening, we dropped off the kids at my mother's and continued the party at home. We invited Smaras, Memos with Anna, and Stathogiannis, who brought one of the chicks he'd been fooling around with lately. We took out a case of Amstel from the inox fridge, laid out ten packs of cigarettes on the coffee table in the lounge and put *Dionysiou* on at full blast. At some point, a little after midnight, there was banging at the door. I open the door and what do I see? Two coppers!

"What do you want?" I said, trying to guess from their lip movements what they were saying.

"There is a complaint made against you for disturbing the peace," shouted one of them.

"By whom?" I asked and sprang to the balcony. Meanwhile, Sotiria had turned down the stereo.

"The neighbourhood," I heard the copper behind me say.

"I'll find out who's the asshole who did this and I'll deal with him. The moment something good happens to you, they want to tear you apart. I never meddled in their shitty lives, I never cared if they had money or not. I never bothered them in any way."

"Oh, come on, you did bother them. They call us all the time for disturbance of the peace," the copper gave me a look.

"They're jealous, I'm telling you, jealous, but I'll fix them. Stratos may be late to respond, but he doesn't forgive."

I offered to treat each to a beer; as it was the opening of my shop and whenever they wanted, they could bring their cars over for a free wash. They couldn't drink; they were on duty.

"Turn the damn thing down, we're in no mood to have you bringing us back," said one of them. I said "fine" and as soon as the police car made a turn to Traleon, I put *Giagkousi* on at full blast, to spite my enemies.

"Turn it down!" Sotiria begged me, but I said that I wouldn't let some cocksucker ruin my day and my party, and I went out singing like Peggy Zina: *"Little boy, have no doubt, if you want to get with me, be yourself and tough it out."*

Chapter 27

On Monday morning I found Simo outside the shop.

"Good morning, Simo, how are you?" I said, and leaned forward to unlock the shiny padlock of the front garage door.

"Good morning, mate. I'm here to work," stuttered Simos.

"Work where?"

"At your shop. My mum said you might need an assistant, so I came."

"I haven't even started yet; I can't afford an assistant! We'll see how it goes. Let me make some money first and we'll talk about it."

"You don't have to pay me, I'm on disability. My mother said that, if you don't mind, I could come and pass the time."

"If that's the case, welcome," I said, and I sent him out to get me some cigarettes.

From then on and until I kicked him out, Simos would come at the time I opened, leave briefly at noon and return in the afternoon and stay until closing time. He was like my sheepdog. In addition to the cigarettes, I would send him off to the avenue to see if any car was coming and bring me down my lunch from Mrs. Nickie.

I started with great enthusiasm and, as we all know, enthusiasm for work is what generates work. At first, my job smelled like grease, car detergent and wax. I feasted my eyes on the fuchsia and yellow brushes of the automatic washing machine which span around their axes and the cars. I couldn't get enough of hearing the automatic beaters slapping the carpets "pat, pat." The only real dampener were the customers who had the bad habit of standing behind me and telling me how to clean the windshield, how to wipe the upholstery and how to lubricate their clunker.

"Why are you hovering over me like the Grim Reaper?" I said the other day to an old chap, an ex-HMRC employee.

"Why? Do you mind if I want to stay close to my car?"

That clunker, big deal, I thought.

"You don't have to be here. Your car is in good hands. Go have a cup of coffee next door," I said.

"I'm off coffee, I have high blood pressure," replied the prick and cleared his throat.

"Have an orange juice then and when I have the Kadett ready, I'll give you a shout."

He sat there for a moment looking at me. Then he took a few paces back and forth on the pavement and eventually decided to leave.

"Go to the girls, old chap, and when your clunker is ready, we'll let you know," said Simos. Luckily, he was hard of hearing and didn't catch what he said.

I could understand the old chap's hesitation, for I know all too well the longing of the Greek man, who would rather loan his wife than his car, and who wouldn't trust you with the keys to his convertible unless you ranked very high on his scale.

As soon as the old man got his old banger, I made a deal with Koula to give me coffee at half price. The following day I added an extra three euro to the price of the car wash, with one Greek coffee on the house, and managed to get every prick who owns a junk car and thinks he is world leader off my back.

On Fridays and Saturdays, Saint Antoniou was filled with double-parked cars. The entire street, from the beginning of Irakliou to Nea Ionia, was mine. In one month, I paid up the tiles and in two months, the electric shutters. It was the best job I ever had. I didn't have to pay rent, and the cost of lights and water was handled by Mrs. Nickie. When I left in the evenings my pockets were full. At home, Sotiria would count the bills shouting exclamations: 10, 20, 30, 100... By Easter, I was washing twenty cars per day, not to mention the oil changes.

Chapter 28

Two months passed and it was almost time for Taratselis to call me for the roof in Varympompi. It was imperative that I found a trustworthy and hard-working assistant to fill in for me on the days I was at the construction site. I told my aunt Koula and a couple of customers to keep an eye out. Nothing. Until one day, on my way to the cemetery to pick up some chipped marble–I was thinking of laying the backyard of the shop myself–I got myself an assistant, a Syrian man named Sakis. I found him over a dumpster in front of the main entrance.

"Dig all you like; you're not going to find food in here. The dead neither cook nor eat," I said and he looked at me quizzically. "Do you want a job?" I asked and he shook his head. "Come with me," I said and took him to Paranda. I bought him a cup of coffee and a cheese pie and when he got stronger, I took him to the shop, where Stathogiannis' Black Beauty was waiting to be washed. Sakis walked up to the car, looked at it from all angles, stroked the back bumper like he was stroking a chick's ass and then he wiped the car clean. He was quiet, but he worked like a dog.

"Well done, you're cool and passionate," said Stathogiannis and tipped him five euros.

"Why did you bring that black guy here? Am I not good enough for you?" asked Simos, looking askance at him.

"You're in general duties, you're a manager," I reassured him.

I had Sakis working from morning to night for ten euros, tips not included. It was more than enough.

Chapter 29

From March to summer, I worked bloody hard, but then I made big money. All day long I felt a red glowing ball bobbing up and down inside me going "tap, tap" and in my mind the festive amusement park lights of joy lit up. I walked into the local shops and everyone knew me and treated me to something. Even Blue Sky opened on my account one day in late May, when I returned from the construction site to find Sakis washing Dessie's white convertible!

"Whose is it?" I pointed to the car.

A lady had left it that morning and was coming by at noon to pick it up, my assistant tried to explain.

"Why are you asking that idiot? He doesn't know. It belongs to Mararas' wife," chimed in Simos, who was smoking one of my cigarettes in the office. I was about to give him a proper bollocking, but there was no time, because Dessie came in. Congratulations and well done and what a beautiful shop, the most modern in the area, she complimented me and picked up her car saying that from now on her whole family would bring their cars to me. I stood gaping at her. I was now a gentleman with a capital G, I had become Somebody!

Meanwhile, summer was just around the corner and Sotiria's leave was coming up. We decided that, after all these years, it was time for a family vacation. Nickie was turning six and Nikolakis was already a year and a half old. Sotiria wanted to go to Paros, but we were unable to find tickets.

"Don't worry, darling. We'll go next year. Find somewhere else to go," I said to her.

Sotiria, who stops at nothing and when she gets an idea she follows through with it, asked her girlfriends and her bridesmaids and finally found a two-storey flat in Meganisi for 150 euros per night. We packed our stuff and off we went. "You're in for a treat, darling," I told my wife, accelerating on the national road and she felt me up while peeking at the children.

We arrived late in the afternoon and hung out at a tavern. The kids went into the water, which was a faded indigo colour. We collected them with difficulty after seven o'clock so as to get to the two-storey flat. Oh, it was posh and splendid! I heard Sotiria chatting with the landlady by the pool, where the water gurgled, and I understood even better what it's like to have money, lots of money, and spend it. We ate like kings, bathed all day long, and at night we would hang out on the veranda, gazing at the lights of the boats that slit the murky body of the sea that buzzed under our feet. We stayed an extra five days and we would have stayed longer, hadn't it been for a lawyer who went bonkers over a portion of gyro on pita and was out to get me.

On Saturday night, Nickie wanted souvlaki and the landlady sent us off to a place in Vathi, after calling and asking them to put some gyro aside for us, because, according to her, you won't get any unless you order early. We lounged by the sea and waited for our order, while we had a hard time holding down the boy, who wanted at all cost to climb onto a yacht, that was within a hair's breadth from our table. The lady behind us talked nineteen to the dozen. She was trying to explain to her annoying girlfriend, how beautiful the island was and how peaceable its people were, and she had given us a headache. It was nerve-racking. When the gyros servings came, the lady sees them and starts bitching at the waiter; because, although they had been there before we'd arrived, they were told that the gyros had run out, so where did the gyros they served us come from? The waiter was trying to explain to her that we had ordered it in advance and she talked to him about market regulation authorities and breaking the law. That's when I couldn't take it any longer and I threw the whole table overboard.

"Feed her the bloody cow so she can choke on it; for being on our case for three gyros on pita!" I said to the waiter and took my family and the little one who was crying and left without paying.

In the morning, I found the policeman at our door. I harassed the lady lawyer who was also a municipal councillor of Lefkada, he said to me, and I better pack by noon and get out of there to avoid further trouble. I didn't want trouble either, so we left in a hurry because of the cunt. We were getting bored anyway. Mountains are better than the sea. We spent the rest of the days in Antista, where we did as we pleased and no one dared bother us. After a month we returned to Athens changed persons.

My wife would say the word "Stratos" and her mouth would be dripping honey.

Chapter 30

That year Nickie was going to be in the first grade and on the day of consecration we, as a family, went up to the school on Ioannis Fokas.

"She doesn't like school," I said, watching the girl pulling her mother towards the swings.

"She takes after her father," my mother jumped in.

"Who would you have liked her to take after? The best man or the butcher? The kid is smart and smart kids prefer playing to studying," I said.

"Be quiet," Sotiria poked me. "She can hear you, it will go to her head and then she will not want to go to class."

"Big deal, it's not as if she is missing out on college," I said, seeing my old school, the same schoolyard, the same windows, the same puddles, the same flower beds. Nearly thirty years later and nothing had changed there.

The schoolyard was bursting with parents and children. Nickie found two or three kids from kindergarten and ignored us completely and the little boy tried to tear himself loose and jump out of the stroller. At approximately ten o'clock the teachers came out to the schoolyard and I was left with my mouth hanging open.

"What's wrong?" Sotiria asked.

"That's Socrates!" I said."

"Who?"

"Socrates is still here."

"Who is Socrates?" she asked.

"My teacher. It never even occurred to me that he would be alive after all these years."

And yet, not only Socrates was there, but he took the microphone and made a speech. I couldn't believe my ears. It was as if I had fallen into one of the holes you see in science fiction movies and have ended up in a parallel universe. After half an hour of Socrates' bullshit–a leopard cannot change its spots–the consecration was over and each teacher took their class and proceeded to the halls; that's when I saw her. I saw the Albanian woman who two years ago the contractor had kicked out of Mararas' shack from across the street pushing a toddler in Nickie's line.

"Did you notice the Albanian?" I nudged Sotiria. "Whose brat is that?"

"Her grandson," my mother jumped in.

"She has a grandson?" I asked.

"Yes, it's her daughter's."

"And she will be in the same class as our Nickie?" I shouted and walked over to the strange woman. "Where are you taking the child?" I yelled at her.

She froze and looked at me quizzically, as if she didn't understand what I was saying to her. I then pull the boy out of the line and push him in her direction. He hid in the old woman's arms and they both started screaming. They all turned to face us and looked alternately at the old woman who was tangled up with the little boy, and at me hovering over them and cursing. After seconds of this strange silence, there was a commotion, and before I could say anything, I saw parents, teachers and children heading my way.

"What's going on here?" came the shrill voice of Socrates, emerging from the human wall that formed opposite from me.

"What do you think is going on, teacher? I am Stratos Achtidis, your old student, and I have brought my daughter to school to keep the tradition going. But I see that you have put the Albanian bastard in her class."

The little boy and the old lady started squealing.

"Looks like your boy Stratos hasn't really changed and is still the ray of sunshine he used to be, Mrs. Nickie," Socrates turned to my mother, who was trying to pull me away.

I felt like slapping him, but I restrained myself. Nickie hung on to my belt, crying.

"Ray of sunshine or not, my kid will not be in the same class as the Albanian, teacher."

"You were a plonker then and a plonker now, Stratos." Socrates looked at me from below–being a short-arse man and all–and bit his tongue with his few teeth like when he used to catch Simos and I beating up the kindergarteners; which I did out of my belief system and Simos out of his stupidity.

"In our school there are no ethnic groups and religions. Here all children are equal and have the same rights. If you don't like it, take your daughter to a private school. But I don't think you'll find a school in the whole country that isn't attended by students from other countries."

While the fool was talking, the hags of the Parents and Guardians Association were yammering behind me and calling me a racist. Accordingly, I turned around and gave them the finger. That's when all hell broke loose.

"Why are you calling him names?" a heavy-set man in black clothes and hands full of tattoos jumped out from the bars. "As a pure Greek he has the right not to accept that his child attends the same class as the Albanian kid. If you are fond of the illegals, take them home with you. Not only do they come and take our jobs, they have the audacity to bring their kids to our schools! Not just them, but the Bangladeshis and the Pakistanis as well. You have opened the doors for them to come in and taint our culture and history. They should all go back to their countries, go back to their filth."

The silly cows of the Parents and Guardians Association started yelling and pushing us towards the schoolyard door, Nickie was crying, the boy was banging his head on the sides of the stroller.

"No fascists in our school!" the hags yelled.

"Okay, we'll deal with you later," said the man who defended me and left.

I took my wife and the kids and went out onto the highway, where I caught him starting a Harley.

"Thanks man, for taking my side. If it wasn't for you, those cunts would have eaten me alive," I chimed in.

"I just did my duty to a Greek patriot, and a childhood friend."

"Childhood friend?" I repeated.

"Don't you recognise me, Stratos Achtidis?"

"No, who are you?"

"Have I changed so much? It's Dimitris, Mrs. Polyxenis' son."

I couldn't believe my eyes. Dimitris lived on Orfanidou street, in the same block of flats as Smaras and Simos, and I was two years older than him. As a kid, he was the neighbourhood's troublemaker. He used to throw rocks at cars on Irakliou, beat up younger children, break candelabra and marbles in the cemetery and cause damage to the neighbours. Once, with my brother as an accomplice, they drowned ten little chicks that belonged to a woman working in the street market. Later we found out that he got mixed up with two other guys, the likes of him, and pretending to be in a TV crew, they stole an old woman's icons in Kifissia. They were caught and sent to a juvenile detention center. From then on he disappeared without a trace, until the day he showed up at school, like deus ex machina to side with me.

"How many years has it been since we saw you, Dimitris! What have you been doing?"

He told me he had some run-ins with the law, he went to juvie and then to prison, he got married and had a child. Afterwards he lost his job, because of the foreigners, his wife left him and he took his son and moved to his mother's. It was the kid he had brought to school that day.

"Notice how, except for the silly cows of the association and that prick, the principal, no one else spoke? No real Greek wants foreigners. They're just scared of the liberals, what's that about, and they don't speak up. But there is indeed a movement, friend, there is a movement," he said. He asked about me and I introduced him to Sotiria, I told him about the Tsunami and invited him to Parada to have a cup of coffee, my treat. He said he would love to come, but first he would treat me to one at a cafeteria in Saint Eleftherios. We arranged for him to pick me up from the Tsunami that same afternoon.

We returned home with sullen faces.

"And now what do we do? Why do you have to be so obnoxious? How can the child show up to school now?" my mother asked.

"Mind your own business. This is our child and she is not going to be in the same class as the Albanian boy," Sotiria jumped in.

"It may be your child, but when you're at work and Anna is on her day job, I'm the one who babysits," my mother sassed.

They nearly started a catfight right in front of me.

"Come on you two, collect yourselves," I intervened. "All this time, I've been boasting about mother-in-law and daughter-in-law getting along fine, and now you're about to quibble over trifles."

"You call the child's school quibbling over trifles? My mother looked at me red-faced.

"Mother, I'm not going to send my child to the same school as the Albanian kid. I will figure something out."

The next day I enrolled Nickie in a private school. I had a few grand saved up, which I spent on my child and my country. Sotiria was in accord with me.

Chapter 31

In the evening, around seven, I heard an engine rev up outside the shop. It was Dimitris with his Harley. I threw my oakum to Sakis who was washing mats in the backyard and got on the bike. Between Agios Eleftherios and Ano Patissia and next to the train tracks is Black Dog, a cafeteria with an attic, black tents and curtains. That attic was the guys' haunt, Dimitris told me proudly, as he pushed his bike between two others of the same make.

"The guys are pretty straight up and above all they are patriots like yourself, with a conscience and a set of balls, mind you," he said and went into the shop, puffing up his muscles like a turkey puffs up its feathers. He offered me a seat at his table and ordered me a frappé.

Before long the attic was filled with heavy-set men all dressed in black clothes, with Greek tattoos on their hands and feet: Greek meanders, Christs, that sort of thing. They started conversing casually about the better days to come and the eradication of unemployment, caused by the foreigners. They all said and agreed that illegals should get out of the country, similar to the old Socialist Party saying "out with the military bases from hell!', given that the enemy was only one: the communists, the proofters, and the illegals, who should get the hell out one way or another so that the sun of righteousness shines again in our country. Then they talked about patrols and vigilance and when

I told them this wasn't up to them, but to the police and the law, they told me that the only law of the land was the law of purebred Greeks. That is when I realised I was in a pretty pickle and that I should keep my mouth shut to make it out alright.

At the time I was neither leftist nor rightist, nor anything. All I cared about was getting by and I didn't care about foreigners unless they poked their noses into my business, like, say, that Albanian woman this morning. I didn't like being in cahoots with Dimitris' friends, even if the police turned a blind eye and gave them a free pass to clean out the place. Nor did I get a say in what they said they were going to do. They can do as they damn well please, as long as it doesn't involve me.

I came home late and for a long time afterwards, every time Dimitris invited me back to Black Dog, I would tell him that I was too busy and I avoided him.

Chapter 32

At the end of October, I got the money from the EEC and at the end of January 2009 I parked Sotiria's cool red convertible on the pavement of Olofitou. I honked five or six times and when she finally came down, I tossed her the keys. She couldn't believe her eyes. "Didn't I tell you I'd get you a new car?" I asked her and she jumped all over me. Memorable moments.

It was drizzling that day, but we put the top up and put *Dionysiou* on at full blast. Revving and honking we drove down to Vathi Square, to a tattoo parlour owned by Dimitris' best friend, and Sotiria got a thunderbolt on the neck, the same as Lola's in Paranda, and I got a meander, which was very popular, on my left calf. First and foremost, I am a Greek.

On Wednesday we took the convertible and I arranged a night out on Saturday with Taratselis and his chicks. Even though mister Nikos is a couple of years younger than my mother and looks like a bag of leaves, he's very well-off and the neighbourhood's hags want nothing more than him taking them out.

Early in the morning he dropped off his car with the instruction to make it sparkle. In the evening, he was going to show it off to a new chick, Lena, a divorcee lawyer from Antista he had his eye on since she was little, but she acted all educated and being the daughter of a schoolteacher she wouldn't go for the unrefined construction worker. However, times changed and Taratselis, with his mud and his bricks, became a big contractor, whereas she was a divorcee without a penny to her name.

"Tonight, we are going to listen to Paola sing. Would you like to take your wifey and come? I have booked a table for fifteen people," Taratselis said.

"Who else is going to be there?" I asked.

"Me, Lena, the girls, the doctor and Jenny, as usual. And mind you, not a peep to your aunt."

"Didn't you guys break up last year in Evangelismos over my bandaged leg?"

"We broke up, we got back together and we broke up again, and I don't want her to hear of my debaucheries. Helen may be your first-degree aunt, but she's my first girlfriend and I don't feel like causing her pain," he said with some difficulty.

"If you swear that you won't lay a hand on Sotiria, I'll be there."

"Taratselis is an honest man and would never touch his niece."

"Oh, come on. You shagged your first cousin who is your own flesh and blood, what's to keep you off your niece?"

"You are hilarious, my nephew," he burst out laughing and stroked my cheek. I threw him the keys and grabbed a fifty.

Aside from the fact that he may grope and shag your woman, Taratselis is a nice and generous guy. I took the day's collection, gave Sakis his ten euro note and with the "tap, tap" of the phosphorescent ball inside me I went upstairs to Mrs. Nickie.

"Mother, tonight I need you to babysit so I can take my wife out," I told her as she served me the moussaka.

"Will Sotiria be okay with that? We haven't talked to each other since the day we took Nickie to school," she said.

"She'd better," I said and started eating. "Mrs. Nickie, you're such a great cook. There is no match for you."

"And where are you taking her, my son?" she asked.

"To Paola, along with Taratselis, the doctor and his..." I bit my tongue.

Mrs. Nickie leaned against the sink and stared at me, her eyes the colour of an olive tree during the first rains. She then crossed me and spat on me three times.

"Let Jesus and the Virgin Mary guide you, my son. You have finally found your way. You have a family. You have a good wife, who is able, never mind my disagreement with her. Brides and mothers-in-laws are like cats and dogs. She kept you on the straight and narrow and I am proud, because I can't expect anything from your brother," she lowered her voice so as not to be heard in the lounge where Lefteris was snoring, "who's exactly like your father."

"Don't worry, mamma, your son is here for you, as you've always been here for him," I hugged her, and while she was getting ready, I ate the moussaka and cleared the table for her.

At the strike of eleven I went down to the garage with my wifey.

"You drive," she threw me the keys and there was a sparkle in her eyes. She was wearing her white lamé dress with the black tights and she was markedly taller than me with her silver four-inch heels. Her loose hair glistened in the industrial light of the garage, just like the sheet metals on Black Beauty. Her only flaw was the front tooth that slipped through her bright red lips and made her lisp.

At the corner of Traleon and Veikou, Jenny and two of Taratselis' chicks–I can't even recall their names–were waiting for us. There was traffic on Veikou, congestion on Protopapadaki and Katechaki, but on Karea Avenue the traffic flow was smooth. From the back seat, Jenny started her usual bullshit about how she got a job as a secretary for Socrates' son, the paediatrician, getting fifty euros per month, and I told her that fifty euros per month was next to nothing and she started saying that the amount was symbolic, since they were seeing each other and he had promised her to divorce his wife to marry her and that he worshipped her, and that... I have had enough. I turned right onto the corniche.

The road was quiet, so I took the opportunity to challenge to a race a couple of luxury cars, that weren't able to compete with Sotiria's red panther, and ate our dust.

At exactly twelve o'clock, I parked our car outside the club, that flashed like a Christmas tree. The place was sparkling. I tossed the key to the valet and with the chicks on my tail I went straight to the doorman, who was blocking our way with his huge body. "Taratselis," I said, and made him melt like a candle as he took a bow to the ground.

The burly man opened the big double-leaf door with the black leather lining and we stepped inside the holy ground. A practically naked girl led us to Taratselis. Mister Nikos, lounging at the front row table with a pile of carnation baskets in front of him, told us to take a seat. Opposite him, eyes glued to the dance floor, Jenny's paediatrician was sipping his whisky. Paola, within a hair's breadth, was singing with all her might. Every now and then, she would lean to the side to take a flower from Taratselis' hand and blow him a loud kiss with her big lips. That night I drank a bottle of whisky all by myself and sang at the top of my lungs: "*Crazy, who me? Ooh, I drown in my whisky.*"

Sotiria, in high spirits, danced a Zeibekiko and roused the place. That's when that ugly-looking bow-legged guy showered her with flowers and I flipped. "Hey, man, stay away from my wifey or they will have to carry you out," I hissed to him and he turned tail. The brunette Paola in her black bodysuit kept on singing behind a heap of carnations and I, with the cigar that Taratselis had shoved in my mouth, blew her kisses, singing: "*You're crazy, you're crazy to compare me with another, I'm crazyyy.*" Across from me, Jenny was perched in the bald doctor's arms and kept on staring at me.

When Paola sang, "*I wonder*", Sotiria climbed onto the dance floor with a glass of whisky and a cigarette in one hand, and the carnations that this divine creature had given her in the other. That is when Jenny took the opportunity and gestured that she was going to suck my cock and as I was nodding my head up and down, Sotiria catches a glimpse of the movement, and throws herself on the dimwit and she would have pulled her hair out if Taratselis hadn't separated them.

Then everything became a blur. People were passing me by with huge smiles and it was as if I was running down the highway at full speed. The music was pouring into my ears and billowing like a rogue wave. I could sense the club, the lights, the people and the tables spinning around and Paola flying towards the ceiling with her hair moving like black snakes. *"You're crazy, you're crazy"* came her voice from near and far, and I plummeted in the back seat of the convertible, as if I had fallen off the seventh storey. Sotiria started the engine and I sang *"I'm crazy"*, with the wind slapping me in the face and ruining my good mood, and saying "Mother of God, where are you taking me?" And every now and then I stuck my head out of the window and barked.

"Sit down and put your head in; you're bladdered again," Sotiria shouted.

We arrived home at day-break. My mother started yelling:

"You're back to this again? And you, Sotiria, how come you let him get so drunk?"

"Stratos is a big boy and he can look after himself. But don't give him a hard time for taking it a little too far tonight. He deserves it," she said.

I was flat on the floor with my back to the front door, singing: *"I'm crazy, you're crazy to compare me with another"* when I smelled plain Greek coffee from the kitchen. Coffee is to the drunk what holy water is to the devil.

"Come, drink some to get your wits about you," Mrs. Nickie hovered over me, with a yellow nightgown on.

"Do you support AEK club?" I asked her.

"No, Panathinaikos," she replied laughing.

"In that case, I won't drink it," I said and sealed my mouth.

They forced a couple of sips down my throat and I went to the bathroom. I came out and as I was headed to the sofa, I heard Sotiria's complaints:

"Enough with you already. You pissed in the bathtub again."

"*I'm crazy, you're crazy*" I said, and the "tap, tap" of the fuchsia ball inside me grew exponentially, before I passed out.

Chapter 33

The Sunday following the shindig at Paola's was a tough one. From the time I opened my eyes at ten o'clock, I was crawling from the sofa to the bathroom and from the bathroom to the sofa, with a headache piercing my skull like a cold needle. And as if all this wasn't enough, Sotiria left for work at one o'clock and left me with Nikolakis and Nadia, the daughter of her dinner lady friend with whom she shared shifts. The girl was a year older than our own pride and joy, and Sotiria, who longed for the boy to socialise more, pressured her mother into bringing her around often for a playdate, which usually ended with them beating each other up.

At around two o'clock I fed the rascals with the *tarhana* that Sotiria had prepared and let them play ball and beat each other up on the balcony. We were amid those glorious *Alkyonides Days* and the sun was blazing. I was fast asleep, when at around four o'clock there was thunder and lightning. It was one of those rain showers that come out of nowhere and drown people, and then cease as abruptly as they came and the rainbow comes out.

I got up with difficulty to get the two rascals who were dancing in the rain screaming, when on the balcony's roof flickered the blue light of a police car that had pulled over across the street. "Inside, quickly," I pushed the kids to the lounge and pulled the balcony door. With a towel I was trying to dry the brats who couldn't stop flinching, when the intercom rang. They were downstairs. If I find out who's the bastard that tipped them off, I'll hang him upside down, I thought to myself, and I told the kids who were dancing on the sofa to put a sock in it. The coppers rang a couple more times and seeing that I didn't let them in, they scrammed. Good riddance, I said through clenched teeth.

It was half past five when to my horror I realised that it wasn't for another full five hours before Sotira was due to return with her friend to collect the brat. I opened the door wide and put *Paola* on at full blast. "*You're crazy, you're crazy, ooh*" and went outside to see the mice pacing back and forth in their cages with the awnings rolled down. I was annoying them and it felt good. After I played the same song about a dozen times, I hung over the railing and yelled at the top of my lungs that I was going to shag the bastard who calls the police on me every now and then.

The little girl was frightened and let out a shriek. I looked at her crying like a piranha with her pointy white teeth and I barely kept myself from punching her in the face. I told her to shut up or I'd take her out onto the street where the wolf would eat her, and after I put on a CD with wolves and little red riding hoods for them, I lay on the sofa until Sotiria and her friend came and found me sound asleep and the kids all smeared with *Merenda* eating my cigarette butts. They laughed with the kids' accomplishment and didn't even think to scold me. In the evening, Sotiria and I each drank an Amstel on the balcony and then we bonked all night. When you have money to spend on their behalf, women don't complain about anything; they forgive everything and they let everything pass.

Chapter 34

First thing Monday morning, Jenny's paediatrician and Socrates' son came by the shop.

"I passed outside this place every day and I didn't know the Tsunami was yours, and I would have never known if Taratselis hadn't told me the other day, at Paola's."

"And I would never have figured out that you are the teacher's son. How was I supposed to recognise you, when you've changed so much since school?" I said to him.

He dropped off a brand-new Saab 9-5 with white leather seats fully equipped, and he said he would come to pick it up at noon after work. It was Sakis' day off and I had Simos vacuum the cabin, while I cleaned the boot. The stuff that was in there was unbelievable. From thongs to bras and condoms. Apparently, he had turned out to be a womaniser; that slug who was four grades ahead of me in school, who used to slurp his snot that ran down his nostrils like spaghetti. And who, during recess, instead of playing, would hang out in the shade of the acacia and do next hour's homework. When you become a doctor, it doesn't matter how much of an arsehole you were in school. People respect you, everybody calls you "doctor, doctor" and you look at them over your glasses as if they are extraterrestrials. As for the women, they see a white coat and have an orgasm.

At about eleven I parked the Saab on the pavement across the street and went for a cup of coffee at Paranda.

"The usual, mister Stratos?" Lola asked me and wiped the bamboo table with a Wettex.

"Don't mister me. If you want us to get along, kiddo, call me Stratos." I fixed my eyes on her bra.

"Okay, Stratos," she blushed down to the roots of her hair.

I was about to finish half a pack, when I heard shouting and commotion from the Tsunami. I run over and what do I see! Simos beside himself, cursing at our teacher, Socrates.

"Socrates, you are a bloody cunt."

I flew off the handle. The doctor, who had come to pick up his car, in the company of his father, was at a loss for words. Socrates was staring at Simos unperturbed and mocking him like he used to: "Yeah, yeah."

"Put a sock in it, you prick," I grabbed Simos by the neck and kicked him out onto the street. "If I ever see you at my doorstep again, I will make you swallow your tongue for trying to drive away my clientele," I said, flustered, and apologized profusely to the doctor and, for the first time in my life, to that brute, my old teacher who for six years had been breathing down my neck.

Chapter 35

As soon as Simos was booted out, the climate at work changed. It was a big mistake to bring him into the shop. He talked all day long and made my head buzz, not to mention that he acted like he was the one calling the shots and as if he was Sakis' boss.

The following week was a rainy one–how could it not, seeing that it was full blown February. Monday morning, on my way down to the shop, I found Lola outside the Katerina Supermarket on Irakliou, with four bags filled with coffee and kitchen paper.

"What brings you here?" I posed the stupid question of the week.

"Buying stuff for the shop," she said and her eyes narrowed at my mouth.

"How come you don't go to Sklavenitis, instead of coming to mister Stelios who overcharges?"

"Koula says we should prefer our neighbourhood, in order for our neighbourhood to come to us."

"She's right. But what neighbourhood is she talking about; they are all shitheads."

"I don't know about you, Stratos. The neighbourhood supports us," said Lola hesitantly, while continuing to stare at my mouth; something which turned me on.

"That doesn't concern me. How about the two of us go get a cup of coffee?" I shouted at her just as she was about to cross the street.

"Well, don't we have coffee together every day?" She looked at me puzzled in the drizzle.

"I meant a different kind of coffee, but since you didn't take the hint, bring me my frappé in half an hour," I replied and watched her hair ruffled as she crossed the avenue.

It was Sakis' day off and I was alone at the shop. With nothing to do, I went out to the backyard and applied Vaseline on an old windscreen wiper which I figured I'd put on Smaras' pickup truck, because it was fine, except for a minor wear and tear of the rubbers.

At about ten o'clock, Lola's voice tickled my ears:

"Your order is ready, Strato." She placed the coffee on the shelf above the two car seats that I use as a lounge next to the shop's left garage door. With the Vaseline in my hands, I went inside and the moment I saw her, I started drooling. "What are you doing back there?" she asked playfully.

"Come here, mama, and I'll show you," I said, without expecting her to come. But she came within a stone's throw and I lost my mind. As a result, without thinking it through, I push her to the water closet behind the automated washer and I pull down her black leggings. She wrapped her arms around me tightly and after a couple of French kisses she knelt down, sighing heavily. She unbuttoned my trousers and shoved my cock in her mouth. I was thrilled! Not even Jenny, the deep throat of Patission, had sucked me like that. Delirious and about ready to cum, I turned her over, I slapped her buttocks, that were soft and flexible like rubber, twice, and I licked her round asshole greedily. She screamed with pleasure.

"Don't shout, mama," I said and smeared on her the Vaseline leftover in my hands.

"Give it to me, give it to me now," she begged, and I shoved it in down to her throat and I shagged her with such mastery and with a longing I hadn't felt in years with Sotiria, while I covered her mouth so we wouldn't be heard on the street. When she came, I came too and I buttoned my trousers, as she picked up her thong. She started to leave, but I stopped her, pushed her against the wall, and shoved it in her again. On the way out, I stuffed a twenty in her bra which she absolutely refused to take. "For the coffee. Keep the change," I said. Outside it had stopped raining and a huge, blazing sun had come out.

I walked after Lola who rode her bike sideways, and rolled it all the way down to Paranda and parked on Irakliou, occasionally turning around to see if I was following her. That's a woman for you, man... It took fifteen minutes, and one shag in upright position to make my day. I rested next to the transparent awning of Paranda and watched the avenue head down to Saint Lavras. I lit one of Lola's Camels, who came and curled up next to me like an Angora Cat, and while sucking at the thick heavy smoke, I looked back at the street where the cars were congested and the curses between the drivers were flying around.

"What will you have, my master?" Lola whispered playfully.

"You, mama!" I blew the smoke in her face.

She laughed shamelessly and left when her mistress called her to go take an order. Shortly after, the hottie rode her bike with two coffees on a paper tray and after going the opposite direction, she headed up to the cemetery. I stood watching her until she disappeared at the bend like a pink dot.

Chapter 36

It was the best period of my life. I was successful, with two jobs, money, a wife, children, and an affair. The cars kept coming to the shop and everything ran like clockwork. Then it was Holy Saturday and we celebrated Resurrection as a family in Saint Andreas. At five minutes to twelve and before the "come receive the light" I get a message on my cell phone: "Season's Greetings and Happy Resurrection Day with those you love." It broke my heart. I had everything I loved next to me, except for her playful eyes. We got home at twelve thirty, we did some egg pocking and I put *Vergoules* on at full blast and danced to it however I pleased, while Sotiria, the children, my mother and my mother-in-law clapped their hands.

Near dawn and in less than half an hour after we had called it quits, my mother called me in tears.

"What it is now, mother? You barely left and you call me back, the moment I fell asleep?"

"Come, we've got to go get Lefteris. It's Easter and that good-for-nothing broad kicked him out on the street."

"It was about time," I said and turned to the other side, turning off the phone, which rang again before I could shut my eyes.

"Come down here now, let's go and collect your brother, your flesh and blood," whimpered Mrs. Nickie. I sat up on the bed and lit a cigarette. Sotiria, next to me, didn't even notice.

I hadn't spoken to Lefteris since March 2003, when Mrs. Nickie had her gall bladder removed. We had taken her to the Emergency room with abdominal pains and she was rushed into surgery. Once she was out, my brother and I returned home to get her nightgowns and slippers, since they were keeping her in for five days, and we figured we'd have some *tsipouro*, just for the sake of it. One glass led to the next one and we got drunk and then we started talking about the subject of the bribe which the doctor asked for–nice man–and realised that we couldn't raise enough money, as well as the subject of who between the two of us had given our mother more than he got in return, the situation became heated, we got into a fight and he shoved a kick in my face that sent me to the hospital sharing a wall with my mother, with my eye rolled backwards. The doctors said I had suffered a "blow out." I nearly lost my left eye, and ever since then it is jammed between the bones. Similar to Memos' wife Anna, I turn to the left and I see right, not to mention I have a ton of problems with the chicks, who think I'm making eyes at them.

I swore I would never talk to him again, but mother didn't let go, so in the early hours of the morning we found him like a beaten dog outside his house during Easter Time. Kathraki took his keys and threw him out into the street with a black Russian suitcase, the one with the silver plastic bars in the corners that glow in the dark, and a big rubbish bag with shoes and unwashed socks. I gave him a hug and pushed him and the bag in the back seat and the smell of feet filled the car. Before I closed the door, he patted my crumpled eye and teared up. I cried as well, and so did our mother. Blood is thicker than water. He's my brother, but he drinks like my father and when he drinks, he loses all control.

From that day Lefteris returned home and got settled in the lounge arm in arm with the TV and the PlayStation. He never even bothered to look for a job.

Chapter 37

With a little bit of this and that, time went by. In late May 2009 I went up to Varympompi and assembled Taratselis' roof. It was the last Friday of the month and Taratselis, who would be handing over the keys to the owners the following day, paid us and clocked us out at eleven thirty, to get the familiar shindig started. At twelve the souvlaki and the beers arrived and, like always, we began to eat, drink, and sing. Afterwards, like always, we pissed in all the basins, for the sake of a solid construction. In the end, we put together the last blend in the backyard and, as always, Smaras, Stathogiannis and I, fell into the mud stark naked and danced, as always, come rain or shine, while the rest of them threw loads of sand on us, except for the big man himself, Taratselis, who hosed us all down.

I have never laughed so heartily, I have never enjoyed smoking so much, nor have I ever drunk more without getting drunk than on those Fridays when construction work was over. Of course, after 2004, when we delivered a project, there was a worm of worry nesting in the back of my head for whether there would be another job starting or I would be out of work for months. But that year I had no such worries. Thank God for the Tsunami and Sakis, who managed to keep it running by himself when I was working day jobs.

At about four I made it to the shop a little tipsy, collected the earnings and told my assistant to hurry up with the two remaining parked cars and go clean the WC. I would be coming around later to check if everything was okay, I threatened him. At four-thirty I unlocked the door to my childhood home and stepped into the dim cold hallway. I dumped the bag with my work clothes on the chest bed in the corridor with the brown grey wallpaper which still spewed the smell of mothball and I still can't see why Mrs. Nickie hasn't thrown it in the trash yet. Old people feel sorry about their things. They've accompanied them through good times and bad, and in all likelihood, they'll be dragging them along all the way to the grave. From the sculpted crystals of the sliding door to the lounge I could make out the furniture with its red throws and the silhouette of Lefteris snoring on the three-seater sofa.

The hallway smelled of *briam*. Hot *briam* with feta! You nailed it Mrs. Nickie; my mouth watered. She was opening the oven when I walked into the kitchen. The moment she noticed me she looked at me over her glasses through the fumes and closed the oven. Then she came limping towards me.

"Oh, you're here. I didn't hear you."

"With the cooker hood at full power and the hallway doors closed, I'm waiting for the day when I hear on the news that a thief came in here like a gentleman and took everything you own, including you," I said to her.

She sat down on one of the four chairs of the formica table with the white meadow and the blue and yellow suns. With a striped towel she wiped the thick sweat oozing out of the roots of her whitening hair, took out a cigarette from her Karelia case, which was under the ashtray, and lit it.

"Am I not getting a cigarette, Mrs. Nickie?"

"Here," she pointed casually at the sealed packet.

"I'll have one of mine." I pulled out the Marlboros and I reached for her black lighter, which she snatched from my hand

and threw it furiously on the table. "What's gotten into you, mother?" I asked her.

"Just now my sister was here and told me that this morning the woman who stays on the storey below yours, Mrs. Dimitra, the one with the fishmonger's place on Veikou, was at the hair parlour." She chewed her smoke angrily.

"Well, what of it?"

"While she was dyeing her hair, Mrs. Dimitra complained to your aunt that you have made the neighbourhood a joke and that everyone is up in arms against you for putting the stereo on at full blast during designated 'quiet hours'. They can't put up with you any longer, so a dozen of them are going to call the prosecutor on you."

"They can suck my balls," I said and took a drag.

"Is that all you have to say to me, son, when I busted my ass working in everyone's house in order to make men out of you? And now that you're married and I figured you're off my back, one sleeps in the living room all day and the other has made it so I feel embarrassed to face people."

"Don't say this to me, mother, when I would kill a man for you! You think more of the bitches that go to your sister's parlour claiming this and that, than your son? Is that what your son amounts to, mother?" I flipped.

"Who should I tell it to? I'm telling *you* because I broke my neck to raise you, because I rushed from work to find you in the hospital with broken legs and ribs when you were eleven and you rode your uncle Nikiforos' bike, which he should never have let you near, and smashed it into the guardrail of the avenue. I'm telling *you* because you barely made it through high school and ruined my dream of you getting a higher education, a chance to escape our destiny, to get a break. I'm telling *you* because when you served in the military they sent you off to the borders and you begged me to send you money for cigarettes and find a contact who could bring you to Athens, because you couldn't stand being away in Evros and the mud of the camp, where you didn't even go out, since it was better to stay in the dormitory, than slosh about in red dirt up to your neck. I'm telling *you* because I signed the shop over to you so that you have a steady income, come rain or shine. I'm telling *you* because you got into a fight with your brother and you were brought to the room next door with your eye sunk into a pit of bones, and I had surgery the previous day and I was worried sick. I'm telling *you* because I prayed day and night to Saint George that you would not take after your father and I expected you to compensate me for my suffering. And instead of giving me this joy, you made it so I'm embarrassed to go out and exchange a word with those good-for-nothing, pretend-to-be housewives who don't lift a finger all day long, and are not half the woman I am. You did this to me, when I was both the man and the woman and I worked my ass off to raise you," she said and started crying, dropping her jaw to her chest, with her lower dentures stirred and about to jump out of her mouth.

I stood up and put my arms around her. My feelings were hurt.

"Don't cry Mrs. Nickie, you break my heart. I swear to you on my children that your son will never give you grief again."

She gave me that sad look, the one I first saw when the coppers came to our house to announce my father's death. That is when that wrinkle dug into her forehead, and like a black score separated her two eyes once and for all, rising from the root of the nose until it disappeared in her sparse curly hair.

I was about ten and my brother was four years younger. We were playing cars, I recall, in the hall with the scarce furniture. The upper floor at the time was still unfinished and we lived on the ground floor. My mother was washing her boss's linens in the backyard, when there was a knock at the door. I ran to open to it, and seeing them made my blood run cold. I tried to close the door, but one of them stuck his boot in the opening.

"Where's your mother, boy?" the other one asked me, and Lefteris started crying. He's always been a pussy.

Mother heard the ruckus and came in, wiping her hands on her apron. I clung onto her wet skirt and Lefteris climbed into her arms. With her gaze heavy upon me and the wrinkle grooving a line across her forehead, mother listened to the copper without uttering a word. After a while, she coughed and asked whether we could see father. The coppers said we couldn't, not before the autopsy. My mother abandoned the laundry and stopped fussing over us. The house was filled with female neighbours, food, beautiful odours and incense. In the morning, we took the bus from Kifissos. Mother wore black and sat behind us with Helen, who cried the whole way saying that father was a goddam waste of time and that, if it hadn't been for his drinking, he wouldn't have fallen and hit his head on the pavement and spilled his brains out, and that it would have been better to bury him on Saint Antony's, than having to drag along two young children midwinter.

Late in the afternoon, we arrived in the small country town and spent the night at the house of a distant relative. The coffin was due in the morning and at noon we would be heading up to the village.

"Luckily it's cold and it won't stink," said Helen at one point. Apart for the smell of fried meatballs, there's not much I remember from that night.

The following day we went to the bus station that was in a sandlot behind the public toilets. Next to the lavatory lay my father's black coffin. The place smelled like piss. When it was time, five men loaded the coffin on the rooftop of the bus and secured it with ropes, together with our luggage, our fellow travellers' boxes of groceries and the little henhouses for the turkeys. It was mid-November. People were getting ready for Christmas. The bus started uphill panting and barking at every corner.

The shadows had tilted to the opposite mountain when we reached freezing Antista. My coat was paper thin and didn't keep out the cold. My fingertips had turned purple. I remember grand-father Lefteris taking me into the square's only coffee place and pushing me towards the heater, and grandmother enveloping me in her wide dress. Mother was silent.

Four men carried the coffin on their backs–two of them were the neighbours who had lowered the stretcher with my beaten-up mother years ago, I can't remember the rest of them. We followed the procession all the way home. Half way there we run into my father's parents, who cried and shouted with steaming mouths that my mother was to blame for their son's death. That is when my mother's eyes turned black with anger. After that I don't re-member anything except for the crying of the women who, draped in black clothes like hooded crows, waited for us in the backyard of our house and the traditional funeral *koliva* that Father Pericles gave me to eat so as not to inherit my father's misfortune.

"And Lefteris? What about Lefteris?" Mrs. Nickie asked me.

"I will handle Lefteris." I furiously put out my cigarette in the white plastic ashtray with the gold-plated logo of Assos Papa-stratos.

"Bless you, my child," she said and tears welled up in her eyes.

"Oh, Mrs. Nickie, you'll get what you want. I will be the son of your dreams. Scout's honour," I said and left her crying over the formica table cloth emblazoned with the blue suns and the smell of *briam* hurting my nostrils.

I hurriedly opened the sliding door and turned on the light. The living room reeked of dirty feet and dog breath. I drew the curtains and opened the two balcony doors wide. Lefteris covered his eyes with his right palm.

"Wake up you no good toerag," I pulled the blanket off him.

"What time is it?" he mumbled.

"It's almost afternoon and you're sleeping. Good for you, mister. Only clocks and suckers work," I said and forced him to get dressed. We went down to the Tsunami and I told him to help Sakis finish up the Fiesta that belonged to the kiosk guy. Then I parked the car on the pavement, sent Sakis with the keys to the owner and gave Lefteris ten euros. "From now on, when I'm at the construction site, you will go down to the shop and get paid ten euros, like Sakis. You're my brother, and blood is thicker than water," I said.

"I didn't expect that from you Stratos, to equate me with the Pakistani," Lefteris sulked.

"First and foremost, Sakis is Syrian, and secondly and most importantly, he more than makes an honest living. You better get down to work and cut the bullshit," I told him and tried to kick him, but missed. That brat knew never to let his guard down.

Pumped up, I arrived home at about five, to find that cunt Dessie's bloody dog howling. Sotiria had worked the night shift and was asleep. I left the bunch of keys on the chest of drawers and next to it the pack with the bright green hundred notes. Then I opened a Coca-Cola and went out to the balcony to make sure that the billiards people were away. I took Nickie's sling and some thin nails and lured their dog. When it came out to the railing, barking, I took aim, and even found my mark twice or three times. I sent the dog inside, bleeding. Afterwards I set the table and waited for Sotiria, who got up long after six. When we finished lunch, she put the plates in the sink and saw the money on the chest of drawers. She abandoned the plates and ran to pat the money, laughing, and it was like the old days, all was right with the world. We shagged hard, until we woke up the boy with our shouting. When Stratos, the moneybags, shags, the neighbourhood doesn't get to rest.

Chapter 38

In the evening, we ordered gyros on pita and hung out on the balcony. Life is beautiful when you have a job and a handsome salary, when you have a wife like my darling Sotiria, two children like mine and a girlfriend, who is ready, willing and able–one as fine as Lola. I was capable of killing a man so as not to miss out on all that, not to miss out on that beautiful evening, with Nikolakis stark naked going around in circles like a spinning top, grabbing bits of gyros which he swallowed in an instant. I put *Dionysiou* on, lit a cigarette and stood by the balcony door, standing tall, when from the side of the awning of Mrs. Dimitra from the floor below, appeared the head of her daughter, the would-be lawyer. I went berserk. Inside, I turned up the stereo's volume.

"What are you doing?" Sotiria rushed to turn down the volume to two.

"I'm having fun," I said and turned the knob to nine.

"Turn it off!" Sotiria yelled and tucked Nikolakis who was jumping up and down screaming, under her arm. I turned it down, hung over the railing and kept watching the balcony below.

"What is it, Stratos? What's the matter with you? I would understand if you had been drinking. But, out of the blue? What's gotten into you?"

"What's gotten into me? That cold twat from downstairs."

I sat there and told her word for word all the things that the sourpuss had said about me at the hair parlour, about her threats, and about my mother who felt sad and my own bitterness for not getting to enjoy myself on the day I finished yet another roof. Sotiria stopped fussing with the baby and sat down without prompting. She lit a cigarette, took a deep drag and directed the smoke upwards. After a while she looked at me. Her eyes sparkled so much that I feared she would go into one of her fits, when she suddenly begins shaking and screaming, and breaking every glass object in sight. I sat quietly next to her and waited, a bit anxiously I might say. Sotiria furiously put out her cigarette and said:

"Never mind, I'll take care of the bitch."

The next day my wife came home with a huge plastic pool from *Jumbo*. She took it out to the balcony and she told me to bring an air pump to inflate it. She then filled it with water, undressed the boy and threw him in.

"We have no need for either *Dionysiou* or the stereo. From now there won't be a single person in the neighbourhood able to get a moment's sleep at noon, or I'll eat my hat," she boasted with her devilish grin. And, indeed, from that moment on up to this day, our lad bathes with his pots and pans and his whistles, and hasn't let anyone get any rest on summer afternoons, particularly that bitch, who used to take naps until five o'clock and spend the rest of the afternoon on the veranda smoking and eating.

Dimitra didn't say anything. What could she do, anyway? Call the police on a three-year old? My darling Sotiria is as clever as a fox and she knows how to make things work for all of us. As a matter of fact, that ballbreaker fishmonger from Naxos, who to our disappointment lived below us, was no match for her.

Chapter 39

Summer had arrvied and I couldn't get enough of Lola. I thought about her constantly and she returned my fondness, any way she could. She brought me coffee every day and on Mondays, when I was alone at the shop, she made time for a quick shag. But that wasn't enough for me and I tried to find something more permanent and safer. In mid-June someone told me about EDEN, a nice little hotel on Acharnon, below the train tracks, where you could book a room for a few hours.

One noon I told Lola to wait for me at the church of Saint Barbara. I pulled over in front of her, taking every precaution. We couldn't afford to draw attention to us.

"Where are we going, my darling Stratos?" she asked playfully.

"I'm not telling you, doll. Light me a cigarette," I replied.

We ate in one of the taverns of Chalkidona and drank sweet red wine, the kind that made her eyes sparkle and turned her into a motormouth. We left before five o'clock.

"This way, Stratos," she said when she saw that instead of turning left onto Chalkidos, I went straight.

"Be patient, we're not there yet," I said and made a left onto Acharnon.

I parked in an alley and we went inside the hotel. Lola's eyes were on fire and the black thunder in the nape of her neck was stretched. We took the lift and by the time we crossed the door of number thirty-seven, we had practically taken off all of our clothes.

In that little room overlooking Acharnon we spent our free afternoons together. Once I opened the door, I would forget Sotiria and the children, the bloody women who were our neighbours and their husbands, the weariness and the drinking. I had no use for alcohol those days for I was constantly intoxicated by love! I lived in paradise but inasmuch as every paradise has its snake, soon a venomous snake sneaked into my paradise. Turns out there was a whistleblower who told Sotiria what was going on, and one afternoon she caught us in the act. It's true, over time we had become careless. We went around in the neighbourhood, talking without taking precautions, and to make matters worse, instead of meeting up elsewhere, we used to take off for the hotel together.

So, that noon we had gone to the fair at Saint Barbara and I had bought her a brown backpack, the one she wanted, and an umbrella with red roses. Then we went down to EDEN. Lola was happy with my presents and she thanked me constantly. "So much for presents. You deserve the heaviest pearls," I said to her and put the key card in the door, at which point a black tornado leaped at us. Sotiria! All hell broke loose. She beat Lola up and plucked out a tuft of her hair. She banged my head with her purse, which is always filled with junk, and almost left me for dead. Luckily the receptionist, who seemed experienced in such situations, noticed and rushed to separate us.

It was a torturous month. There was constant fighting at the house, cursing when calling at the shop, and no coffee for me. On Christmas Eve, Sotiria made me swear on our children that I would never see Lola again. And so the crisis was once more averted. Of course, I didn't stop seeing Lola, whom I now shagged in my childhood home after making mother and Lefteris leave. Cheating is like alcohol: once you get used to it, it's hard to give it up. You just have to be careful and not behave like a moron and get busted, like yours truly.

Chapter 40

The year 2009 ended with jealousy and sullen faces and just when I thought that the wheel would turn with the turn of the year, Sotiria and I had our worst fight ever–and this time I was in the right. On Epiphany Eve of 2010, it was getting dark and I had nothing to do, when my phone rang. It was Smaras, telling me to get down to Blue Sky, where he was drinking and playing pool with Stathogiannis.

"I don't really fancy Dessie's sewer," I told him and reminded him in every detail how a few years back Takis had kicked me out of that hole he liked to call a shop and of my dispute with Dessie over that dog I had bent out of shape.

"So what?" said Smaras. "I don't have enough fingers and toes to count the times I've been kicked out, but I'm not giving them the satisfaction of giving up my haunt. It's my money so I can go wherever I please and if they dare throw me out, I will call the tax office and the police on them and leave the place in a shambles. What is there to be afraid of? After all, they're your customers, aren't they?"

"No, they used to be. But know this, my friend, Stratos is not afraid of any arsehole," I said and put on the jeans that were too tight–good times make you fat–and my brown leather boots. Before I went out, I emptied half a bottle of Old Spice on me.

"Welcome," Stathogiannis greeted us. "Where is Sotiria?"

"At home."

"Why didn't you bring her?"

"This is not a place for women." I replied.

"Sotiria is a tough cookie and the shop is just right for her," said Manos, who used to come by the house often at that time and although he was my friend, got along just fine with Sotiria. They had become buddies and I was proud of my wife who was such a tough cookie that my friends loved hanging out with her.

After a dozen or so beers Manos went to take a leak, and the screen of his mobile phone lit up on the table next to his beer glass. I didn't pay attention. I'm not a nosy parker and I don't care about anyone's business. Memos, however, was born a rat and he wasn't ashamed to rummage through our things, our pockets, our drawers. We used to laugh at his quirk and let him do as he pleased. Besides, we had nothing to hide from each other. That being so, Memos took Manos' phone and read the message. Smaras and I continued drinking our beers, when Memos started that cackling laugh of his.

"What's gotten into you, you prick. Why the hell are you laughing?" I gave him a friendly nudge.

"Listen to this, Strato, listen: 'Mano baby, you are relentless. You gave me an unforgettable afternoon. I bow down before you and I'll be waiting. Sotiria.' Hahaha..."

"Which Sotiria?" I asked.

"6907xxx760."

"Oh, you sly devil, you're a scientist. You learned Sotiria's number by heart to mess with me. You're such a plonker." I began to laugh.

"I'm not joking, Stratos," he gave me a dazed grin.

I grabbed the phone and in my drunken stupor I saw Sotiria's number dancing before my eyes. The earth slipped from under my feet. I slumped down on the sofa and waited for Manos, my mate, my alter ego, to return, to walk in with his legs astride, proud and comforted. As soon as he approached, when he wasn't expecting it, I punched him in the face and planted then one kick and another kick to the face, so hard that he bled and passed out. Then I called the ambulance and went up to the house for the rest of it. It was the first and the last time I raised my hand to Sotiria–and I was in the right.

I saw Manos again in the courtroom, where I got off with a small fine, for anyone who defends his honour is not a criminal, but a hero. I sent him to intensive care, but I enjoyed it and proved once again that no one messes with Stratos' reputation. As for Sotiria, she has kept on the straight and narrow ever since. Moreover, she swore to me on our children that cheating was her revenge for Lola. Female minds.

For two years Manos would see me and walk the other way, because I had promised him that if I ever got my hands on him again, he would be in a wheelchair. And so it was, until Smaras died and there, on his grave, we buried the hatchet and turned a new page. I didn't even mind when he and Sotiria hugged at the funeral. Let bygones be bygones.

Manos and I have been together since first grade. It wasn't easy to erase our thuggery, the afternoons when we picked up the girls from the English tutoring class, and later at the technical high school and that literature teacher who called me a narcissist, but I didn't have the guts to hit on her–being a kid, I didn't dare lay a hand on her–even though her whole body showed me that she fancied me–and so many more things. So, we became best friends again and we put the Sotiria incident behind us.

Chapter 41

After Sotiria's cheating, I finally broke it off with Lola. She chased me for a while, and then decided to leave me alone, then left me to start over my life with Sotiria. We were both cheated-upon, and now we were partying again while Notis Sfakianakis performed: I loved setting fire to bundles of twenties on the dance floor for the '*eagle that dies in the air free and strong*' while Notis shouted through the microphone: "Hey, Stratos you're the man!" Next to him I felt like a god.

In the spring of 2010, Dimitris, the son of Mrs. Polyxeni, brought his bike to the Tsunami for the first time.

"It's Saturday today and in the afternoon it'll be parading on Patission with hundreds more. How much do you want to make it look brand new?" he asked.

"For a tenner, mate, I'll make it top notch," I replied and told him to go next door for a coffee, it was on the house.

"I'm not leaving my queen alone in the hands of strangers. I'll stay here," Dimitris sat tight.

I almost blew a fuse, but said nothing–it was his first time at the shop, I couldn't tell him off–so I began to wearily clean his bike. After ten minutes, Sakis finished washing an old Citroën and came to help, but before his sponge had a chance to touch the spokes of the Harley's rear wheel, Dimitris started kicking him. Sakis ran for cover inside and tipped over the bucket with the detergent. I tried to come in between them and, stepping on the suds, fell like a sack of potatoes on the tiles. I tried to get up and slipped again, and I ended up with Sakis picking me up from the right and Dimitris from the left, while he continued to try to kick my assistant at the same time. I sank down into the chair and told Dimitris to take it easy. Sakis took hold of the hose and poured water into the detergent, which inflated the foam up to the ceiling.

"Are you running amok, arsehole?" I asked Dimitris, rubbing my aching left side.

"Man, if you want me to ever bring it back here, tell your black man to stop defiling my bike with his dirty hands," he hovered over me angrily.

"Why? What did Sakis do to you? He is a good kid and a hard worker, my right-hand man. And if you must know, he's from Syria, he's not black."

"He's an illegal, isn't that enough? They came to Greece illegally, they took our jobs, they stole from our houses and they brought all sorts of diseases from their shithole countries."

Sakis, scared to death, hid in the WC and occasionally popped his head out to peek in my direction, eyes wide. I didn't say anything to Dimitris, I just got up and continued the wash despite my aching body. No doubt my back would be bruised. Dimitris continued hovering over me, telling me what to do and what to be careful of, as if it was the first time I ever washed a bike. With my nerves in tatters, I finished half an hour later, got my ten euros and saw him off. He mounted his bike and turned to Sakis who had just come out into the office:

"As for you, redfoot, I'll kick your ass if I ever see you again," he said and revved up.

Sakis cleaned up the shop without uttering a word. At about three o'clock he asked to get paid in order to be off before five, when the white supremacists would march with their bikes along

Patission. God forbid they got their hands on him. It was then I understood which parade Dimitris was talking about. I felt sorry for Sakis, but I also sympathized with Dimitris who had been left without work because of the illegals, those so-called "refugees" and "migrant workers" the animal-lover environmentalist bitches like Dessie called them.

Come Tuesday, Sakis is a no show at the shop. Nor the next day, or the one after that. I was left alone with ten cars daily and five to six bikes of the Black Dog guys, that Dimitris sent my way, and I was up to my neck in work. If I could lay my hands on that dog from Syria I would have beat it to a pulp, but he had sensed danger and disappeared off the face of Earth without a word.

"Seeing that you're out of assistant, take Lefteris, on the off-chance he gets off the sofa," my mother advised me.

"I did mother, the other day as well, but he didn't stick around. I'll pressure him again, but he is sure to shut me down," I said listlessly. I knew well what an open wound Lefteris was. I would rather give him pocket money from afar, than have him under my feet; not to mention he brought me bad luck.

"You're saying that Sakis from Syria didn't shut you down, and your brother, who comes out of a long line of Greek generations, will?" my mother questioned.

So, with a heavy heart I got Lefteris to come again, where he pretended to work until he patched things up with Dimitris and split every chance he got. On Saturdays he would go down to the parade with his moped and most of the mornings he would escort old ladies to the bank to collect their pensions. When I asked him where he was going, he said that he was doing a public service, since the negros had made old people afraid to leave their homes.

Of course, that cunt across the street, Dessie, gave a lecture from her balcony one day to Mrs. Dimitra from downstairs, saying that civilians' safety is the job of the state and that Greek tax payers pay the police to protect them and that we can't indulge white supremacists and make room for fascism. That those black people and their moron kids are not robbers; they came here because they didn't stand a chance and instead of being welcomed in the homeland of Zeus the protector, they met with violence and terror. Apparently, all those people were family men who were forced to leave their countries because of the war, and that, as the crisis deepens, it is possible that we find ourselves in their place, and have no European country accept us and end up being slaughtered like chickens by the Neo-Nazis in Germany.

It was at that point in her rant that I put *Paola* on at full blast, to keep her from infecting the neighbourhood with her bollocks. Muslims are people, what a notion. Where does she get off saying that that they are just like us and how we will one day be in their shoes and how Europeans will not appreciate us and will kick us around, when six years after the Olympics, people still speak so highly about the organisation of the Olympic Games, and about Greece, the country of the campaign 'Together We Can'.

Chapter 42

In the spring of 2010 Sakis took off and no matter how much I looked around for another Sakis, I wasn't able to find one. The situation with Lefteris was terrible. How was I supposed to get him to work scrubbing cars, when he's been sitting around doing nothing his whole life? Plus, he was ill-natured. The moment I left, he would skim off the cash register, leave the shop unattended and go up to the square for drinks until I went to collect him, or his friends brought him home to us bladdered. To say nothing of the jinx – the bad luck he brought with him. Ever since he set foot in the Tsunami, business took a turn for the worse. Surely, the crisis had something to do with that, but mostly it was the neighbourhood's cunts who talked about my dealings with the guys from Golden Dawn and relayed what went on with Sakis and Dimitris as they saw fit, of course. We were up to our ears in propaganda. The women who spent their time watching morning TV shows did only what Mrs. Popi, Mrs. Despina, Menegaki and Father Philodoros told them to do. If someone the likes of Mrs. Dessie spread a rumour about a certain shop, there wouldn't be a soul who would frequent it.

One morning, Lefteris came for work all dressed up.

"You forgot your tie," I said to him and he gave me a wry smile, the kind he hung on his lips and meant we were about to fight.

I knew he wouldn't stick around. At eleven he was going to meet up with Dimitris to give blood for the purebred Greeks.

"What is that now?" I asked.

"Haven't you heard that Golden Dawn will be headed to Gennimatas hospital today to donate blood provided that it will not be transfused to illegal aliens? I will give Greek blood to Greeks alone."

I told him to cut the crap and grab the hose to wash underneath Taratselis' car. Lefteris, who could care less, sat there watching me until a quarter past eleven when Dimitris came by, got a ride on his Harley and vanished into thin air. Keeping my cool, I polished the dentist's Peugeot that used to be white and was now jet black inside-out, and went out to get the floor mats I had laid out, when I saw an illegal in front of the dustbin.

The place was crawling with them and now they were popping up like soapsuds all the way from the Electric railway up to Irakliou. I ignored him, and started cleaning the ashtray. When I came back out, I saw him swaying as if to fall down. If he hadn't looked clean–first time I ever saw a nigger with such a clear skin–I would have kicked him into the rubbish. If it was up to me, I'd fix him and his bloody race for coming to take our jobs and make fools of us on top of it, like Sakis the Syrian, whom I was now prepared to beat to a pulp if I could just get my hands on him.

The shop went dark with Taratselis' shadow, when I heard the voice of Dessie, that cunt which I had to live with day in day out.

"A man, a man!"

Mr. Nikos stood under the half-rolled up left shutter. I dropped the ashtray and went over to give him the keys and get my fifty. The old chap is always generous. Dessie saw us and, forgetting that a few days back I had ruined her lecture on the rights of migrant workers–that's what she called them–she reached out to us and asked for help. We stood under the Tsunami shutters, watching her run towards Paranda. The black man buckled and leaned against the bin before falling to the side. He lay still for a moment and just when I thought he had kicked the bucket, I saw him move, sit on his knees and bend forward, until his head touched the road.

"Good," said Taratselis. "He is in the right place for the refuse lorry to collect him."

"The lorry comes by at dawn and if he's dead, he will stink by tomorrow." I felt sick to my stomach.

"What's the matter, you prick?" asked the old chap.

"I can't watch them, I despise them," I said.

"Then we should call 101 to come pick him up," he said and went to the phone. Meanwhile Dessie came back with a Fanta and a cheese pie, and picked him up with the help of the girl from the pharmacy across the street. They gave him the drink, while Dessie called us again:

"Help, come and help this man, or at least call 999."

"No need to, we've called the police," I replied.

"How can that make him better?" she said and told me to cancel the call, saying that the man would leave. In the meantime, they had seated him on the saddle of an abandoned bike under the acacia psoralea, in the park across the street, and were asking him what was wrong with him.

He began to sob and his black cheeks filled with black tears. He wept black tears! He told them in decent Greek that he had just been released from the detention centre, where he had been taken three days earlier and they let him out when, after his persistent pleading, when they saw he had papers. With trembling hands, he pulled a transparent bag with some papers in it out of his jacket and showed it to them. The pharmacist's assistant brought tickets from the kiosk and they went up to the bus stop to put him on the bus, because if the police were to come, they said, they would arrest him again. It's women like these animal lovers/environmentalists that ruin things for everybody. It's because of them Greece is full of illegals.

Lefteris came back at three o'clock out of his mind and said that the doctors hadn't accepted his blood.

"Why, brother? What's wrong with you? It can't be anaemia, you're like a bull ready for the slaughterhouse."

He told me to cut it out and said that our doctors are crap and instead of supporting Greek people, they advocate for the illegals who are here to corrupt our ancient Greek civilisation. I asked him to clarify and he explained that the moment they proclaimed in the Blood Donation Department that they were only giving blood for Greeks, the doctors and the nurses told them that blood has no nationality. They said that Dimitris had started causing trouble and they called the security guards who kicked them out. I never took doctors for animal lovers. Too much studying burns the brain.

Part
four

Chapter 43

The year of 2010 was almost over and things didn't seem to be going so well. The economy was going down the drain and strikes were an everyday occurrence. On Wednesday, November 17th the students were getting ready to ask for bread, education and freedom–that revolutionary slogan from the '70s–one more time. They have been saying the same old things for years and years, and instead of sitting tight, they would once again go down to the city center and leave it in shambles.

It so happens that, on that morning, a kid got killed on Saint Antoniou. He was at Paranda having coffee with a girl, when a police car pulled up in front of them. The pricks came out to get coffee and they saw that the kid looked uneasy. As a joke, they asked for his ID. He got scared and ran off. They chased after him and when he was about to turn at the corner, they shot him. The neighbourhood took to the street and the balconies. My aunt saw the kid, all covered in blood, fall on the glass partition of her salon and she fainted. When I arrived, he had already been collected and the girl was crying in her mother's arms who, instead of slapping her for bunking off school, was coddling her. Paranda's door was closed and Lola and Koula's husband were pinned to the window and watching, frozen. I opened the shop and pulled out the hose to clear the blood from the pavement.

"It's forbidden!" shouted the copper from the police car, that was parked right up on the pavement.

"So what? Are we supposed to leave blood at our doorsteps to attract the flies?" I asked.

"They killed Thanasis and you're nagging about the flies?" the girl barked.

"Thanasis had it coming. What were you doing in the cafeteria at this hour? They ought to have killed you too," I said, and the brat passed out.

As if two fainting spells in one morning weren't enough, the radical Dessie arrived with her theories, to act as a lawyer to the dimwit that got the short end of the stick out of his own stupidity. I flew off the handle. No matter what I did, no matter where I went, she was always in my way. As a little boy, I remember her shacking up with Takis, who threw us out of our basketball spot on Labrini square, in order to feel that cow up. Later they got the pool hall at Akrothoon, they named it Blue Sky and she went and sat behind the counter smoking and serving tainted liquor with an air of absolute authority. The moment I bought my flat, she came to live across from me at her father's-in-law, the same she used to call an old prick and couldn't even stand the sight of him when he was alive.

"It's a crime. Murderers, you killed the boy!" she cried out, pulling her hair.

"He had it coming. What was the bloody kid doing in Paranda bright and early Mrs. Dessie?" I lashed out when the coppers finally let me hose down the pavement.

"You have a nerve saying these things, when you make such a ruckus in the neighbourhood that nobody can get any rest. Has the idea that this could be your kid ever crossed your mind?" She took the opportunity to let me have it.

"If my child was playing hooky, I wouldn't wait for the coppers, I would have killed him with my own hands. As for the boy, they said he talked back and it served him right," I answered, increasing the water pressure to clean the tiles.

"And it's the coppers' right to kill whomever talks back to them?"

"What could they've done, Mrs. know-it-all? Let any toerag speak out against them?"

"You're not in your right mind. Who said the coppers have the right to shoot whomever they please. Arrest him, yes, send him to court, yes; but execute him? This is unthinkable in a country where the death penalty has been abolished since the post-war period," she said and stopped talking to me.

The neighbours who hadn't come down to the street shouted at her from their balconies not to pay attention to a fascist like me. I mouthed a "fuck off, all of you," and stepped inside to wash Mr. Vangelis' Toyota model of '92 with only 12,500 miles on it. I've said it a thousand times and I'll say it again: when you see a white Toyota Corolla you flee, because nine times out of ten the civil servant who drives it only takes it out on the road on Sundays and can't tell the gas from the brake.

I finished around twelve thirty and waited for the micro-biologist to bring the jeep, as we had agreed the day before. The clock struck one, the clock struck one thirty: nothing. I saw her as she was leaving and asked her why she didn't bring the car, and she said she changed her mind and would wash it another time. The next day she came and parked almost across the street from me. The car was shiny. She had definitely taken it elsewhere, and only because Mrs. Dessie had made sure that no one in the neighbourhood would want to lay eyes on me anymore. I was going to fix her, though; I had a bone to pick with her. It was common knowledge that on certain nights after midnight the red curtains were drawn and the pool hall turned into a gambling house. Many fortunes changed hands on the green felt of those tables they had out back. I would keep my ears open to notify the police and the Financial Intelligence Unit to catch her in the act and shut her down.

But, according to my aunt Helen, who reads Coelho; the guy who has the women of the world excited with the phrase: "When man plans, God laughs", or something like that, I too was expecting one thing and would get another. Business was slow, I didn't go on vacation during the summer and in September I threw the cat off the third floor. So, instead of Dessie falling into my hands, I fell victim to her libel, once again.

Chapter 44

The year 2011 arrived and everything appeared to come to a standstill. In the shop I was twiddling my thumbs and of course it wasn't just the crisis to blame, but also the incident with the black man, my dealings with Dimitris and the demise of that brat. I dared speak my mind and I was blacklisted by every wannabe Mrs. Dessie, and the neighbours just stopped coming by: they were all anarcho-communists who wouldn't tolerate a business run by a racist, a collaborator with white supremacists like I was. Wasn't what they did to me, racism and bullying?

On top of all that, I had a fight with Taratselis and lost my guaranteed fifty of the week. I got into an argument with him sober and threatened him that if he came near my mother again, I'd rip his guts out. All because he and my mother went up to Zeppelin one afternoon to discuss my aunt, who'd got word that he was involved with a slut from Kato Patissia and had kicked him out of the salon once again. They had their coffee and talked and then, instead of bringing my mother back, he took her to the quarries to make a pass at her. It was there that Mrs. Nickie snapped and gave him a couple of slaps. She told him straight that she wasn't going to sit there and let him shag her, at the place where others shagged his wife, before she sent him packing, for being such a prick.

They returned at about seven and my mother went upstairs almost without a word. Taratselis told me to wash the BMW which was all muddy, and went to Paranda. When I finished, I told my brother to get him. He came, he paid, he took the keys and handed a twenty-euro tip to Lefteris, who looked at me suspiciously, and hastily stuffed it in the pocket of his torn trousers.

"Why are you looking at me like that, you sorry excuse for a man? Think I'm going to steal it? It's yours. The old chap gave it to you," I said.

I didn't like the fact that the prick left all that money. I didn't like the fresh mud on the BMW wheels–there's asphalt in Attiko Alsos–or the fact that he reeked of patchouli from miles away, or the look on my mother's face. After work, I went upstairs to find out what had happened. She said nothing.

The next day, bright and early, I went upstairs before I opened the shop, and I pushed Mrs. Nickie into telling me about the quarries. I went ballistic.

"I'll rip that manwhore's guts out. I'm going to kick the shit out of that bastard for trying to make a pass at my mother!" I slammed my hand on the table and stepped out in a daze.

"Strato, Strato, come back, my child. Come back before it's too late," Mrs. Nickie ran after me.

I didn't listen to her, instead I went to the construction site on the ring road. I found the fatso giving instructions to the workers with an iced coffee in his hand.

"Come on out, I want to have a word with you," I said to him.

"Whatever you have to say to me you can say it here. Taratselis keeps no secrets from anyone," he answered, scared stiff.

"You call yourself a man? The sluts of Patission aren't enough for you, and now you're after my mother?"

"Respect. I forbid you to talk to me like that," he said with the cigarette shaking in his hand.

"You forbid me?" I said and grabbing him by the waist I hung him upside down from the window, facing the cliff. He could hardly breathe.

"Strato, Strato!" the workers rushed in and pulled him inside.

Drenched in coffee and all yellow, Taratselis collapsed on the concrete.

"Mind you, if you go near her again, I will cut your tool off. Keep your hands to yourself, for you'll be in deep trouble with me."

I walked the three floors down, pushing through his employees, who'd all heard the commotion and rushed in to see what was going on.

From that day on my life began to unravel little by little, like a poorly made sweater. Money became even more scarce, it was difficult to repay the loan, Sotiria once again started ignoring me and the children became savages. I asked Nickie where she was going–she was nine years old and roamed around the neighbourhood at all hours–and she would give me cheek: "What did you say, Stratos boy?" Her mother, you see, instead of scolding her, was proud of her behaviour. Since I couldn't even come up with the six hundred for the loan installment, I was useless, I had no say in the family.

All the time, Sotiria complained that she was tired of work and travelling on public transport, now there was no money to spare on petrol, and that she was both the man and the woman of the house. And she had me, a full-grown man, do the cooking, the sweeping, the mopping, and take the boy to the nursery and back.

One day my mother found me cleaning greens and all hell broke loose. She called Sotiria on her mobile and said she better not turn her son into a little woman with a headband that cooks for her and washes her panties, and that next time she better think twice before making me do female chores. Then she took it out on me: "You're an Achtidis, and you let your wife walk all over you? I never expected you to become chicken-liver," she said.

When Sotiria came back, it got messy. She started smashing everything around of her and cursing. She told my mother never to set foot in the house again and she told me that if she ever caught me talking to her, she'd cut my dick off. From then on and for a long time afterwards, I would sneak out to my mother's and she would watch the children from afar, overcome with grief.

Chapter 45

Irakliou avenue rises and dips down like a double grey slug of asphalt, leaving seven-storey blocks of flats on the upper side and half-derelict detached houses on the lower, those that never made it to concrete when times were good and will crumble away, neglected. It's ten thirty and so far, no client has come to the shop, nor am I expecting any. Those with money show up at the end of the week to wash their Mercedé–that's what they call it–so as to flaunt it in the after-hour clubs, where an expensive car can get you laid even with a fake ring.

"What's up Strato? How's business?" Koula asked me when she saw me enter Paranda.

"What business are you talking about, Koula? After the recent price escalation, no one takes the car to go to the news-stand. They think twice before turning the key on the ignition and before paying twelve euros for a car wash."

"That's true," Koula made a sour face and went in to roast coffee for Mr. Stavros, the shoemaker who lived across from me.

"Hey, Strato, isn't that your uncle, Mr. Nikiforos?" Mr. Stavros pointed towards the street.

"Yes, that's him," I replied, after I waited a while to make sure that the red tricycle slowly descending the avenue was my father's brother's wreck.

"Well, wasn't he in prison?" Mr. Stavros wondered.

"They let him go. He was innocent."

"Nikiforos was innocent? Sounds like a joke," he shook his head.

"It was Mrs. Tasia's brats, I tell you, who got him into trouble."

"I'd like to know who got whom in trouble," said Mr. Stavros and before he could finish his sentence my uncle, who had arrived in the meantime, pulled over his wreck next to Lola's moped. I saw him touch her cheek and she burst out laughing.

"Hands off, uncle, she may be good enough to eat but she's jailbait," I laughed.

"She's just right for my new dentures," Nikiforos showed me his teeth and greeted Mr. Stavros.

"Are you out?" he asked him impudently.

"Yes, I am," said Nikiforos and lit a cigarette.

"How come? Didn't they find three kilos of heroin on you?" Stavros prodded him again.

"It was Mrs. Tasia's kids, my poor housecleaner, who took her keys and hid the stash in my refrigerator. And then the Drug Enforcement Agency found it and they locked me up, until those bloody kids confessed and I was in the clear."

"Oh, so you got off easy again," Stavros insisted.

"If you want us to get along, drop the innuendos." Nikiforos ostentatiously patted his pocket and ordered a Greek coffee straight up. When the coffee came, he took a sip and asked about Smaras: "I've been looking for him for three days to transport one of the refrigerators that the Olympic Games organisation gave to the Association of Antisteon and he doesn't answer his phone. Can you tell me where the dirty skunk is hiding?"

"I haven't seen him in a while. He's probably working, I have no clue."

I didn't take the time to explain to him that Smaras had written me off when he found out I was hanging out at Black Dog: "Keep away from the fascists, my brother," he had told me.

I snapped and told him that I didn't like him badmouthing my customers: "The people you call fascists bring me their bikes to wash and now that the market is dead, it's the only way I'm making ends meet." "A dirty ends-meet. Did you forget about the posters of Domnakis we used to put up in Nea Ionia and us listening to Dire Straits from morning till night?" he asked me whiningly and I responded that the period of Communist Youth has been erased from my mind for good and that money has no colour, no matter where it comes from. That's how we lost touch.

"Why don't you call him and see if he picks up?" Nikiforos insisted.

What have I got to lose? At the very most, he's going to curse at me, I thought to myself and rang him. "The subscriber's phone is probably turned off..." came the female voice of the answering service.

"I've been hearing the same thing three days now and if I don't hurry, someone else will run off with my refrigerator," Nikiforos said angrily.

"Hey, Koula, have you seen Smaras today?"

"He hasn't shown up in over a week. He used to come for coffee every morning around seven, before work. His absence surprised me too," said Koula.

I had her call at Blue Sky and IZO. They hadn't seen him in over a week. By this point, I was sick with worry.

"I'll stop by his house and see what's going on," I said and stood up.

"I'm coming with you." Koula tossed her black apron on the counter and followed me.

We walked down Irakliou and turned right onto Orfanidou. At the entrance of Smaras' block of flats, his pickup truck was parked on the pavement with a thin layer of dust on it. We rang the bell, there was no answer. We rang again, nothing. We were about to leave when the door opened and Simos came out. Koula asked him about Smaras. He hadn't seen him in a while, the moron said. The three of us went up to the roof. Simos tried to make small talk a couple of times, but I didn't answer him so he kept his mouth shut.

The door to the studio was ajar. I pushed it open and it grunted. The stench of carcass swept over us. We stepped inside and found discarded pizza boxes and beer tins all over the floor. The two-panelled closet in the hallway behind the door had its doors wide open, the big cracked mirror stood in front of us, the room on the right with the bed unmade, and Smaras hanging from a thick nail on the wall. I passed out.

The following days were bleak. A funeral, a grave, an upside-down burial, no chanting, and a *why,* why did my friend, my mate, the best man in the world do that...? It took me over a month to pull myself together and get back on track.

Chapter 46

A wooden cross and a cheap plastic vase with a handful of wilted flowers are the only ornaments on Smaras' grave. My best friend's grave looks dirt poor next to the black granite slabs, the crystal candelabras, the Murano flowers, the poems and the photographs. Poor and marginalised in life, poor and disdained in death was the illegitimate child of Mrs. Stavrina, who scraped by cleaning graves and lighting candles until her dying day. Almost every afternoon, I went to water the plant and light a cigarette. "Why did you do that, man? Why didn't you say anything? Why, why, why..." I cried buckets.

A few days before his forty-day memorial, a priest was giving a Trisagion service at the adjacent grave.

"Can you come and chant for my mate, too?" I pointed at the grave.

"Suicides don't get chanting," he answered, annoyed, and shook his incense burner.

"Why isn't it allowed, Father? Doesn't he have a soul?"

"He committed the greatest sin. He removed the life the Lord gave him. It's better for his soul not to be commemorated. The Most Merciful One will see that we are not honouring him and He Himself will have mercy on him," the priest crossed himself arrogantly.

"Answer me this, Father. Why does the church allow a dozen bishops to chant for one who walks into a coffee shop and with a firearm spreads death to a dozen homes, and not chant for a man who has taken his life without harming a soul? Answer me, Father, which of the two is more sinful, and who should you chant for, the first one or the second?"

"These are not fitting questions for a man of the cloth," said the priest and he started to leave, dragging his cassock, his overweight body and his incense burner. I jumped like a feline around the graves and caught up with him in the corridor. I grabbed him by the arm and hauled him over Smaras' plot.

"Father, I want to hear *everlasting be thy memory* loud and clear."

He realised I wasn't joking and chanted as he ought to.

Chapter 47

A monotonous life. I haven't had a customer in over a week. The bloody phone hasn't rung in five days. I have running costs. Apart from my mother, no one cares about me, and Smaras is six feet under. I don't care about anyone either. They can all fuck off.

When it's not busy, it's hard to get through the day. The night too. I could go through the whole Athenian Brewery and still be unable to pass the time. I drink and watch TV, I drink and smoke, I drink and sleep and don't give a damn about Sotiria and her nagging. Every day she hides her money someplace else and every day I rummage through her wallet and take what I need for drinks and cigarettes. Every day I go to Paranda, though I resent the way Lola dumps my coffee in front of me and walks away subtly wiggling her round buttocks, giving the impression that my stare bothers her. But what bugs me more is that, despite everything that has happened between us, she continues to turn me on. It's impossible to get the image of picking her up in the bar out of my mind, and I constantly remember her cries.

At night, I turn off the light and with the shutters open I drink, smoke and watch TV until I fall asleep. The window is open, I'm not afraid of the thieves who work double time during the economic crisis. I just wish one of them would make the wrong move and waltz on in, so I can fuck him up.

One night I heard a "bang" outside. I go out and what do I see? The car that belonged to the professor on the third floor, above Dessie, next to the pyjama-man, bumped against the abandoned Volkswagen across the street. She had forgotten to pull the handbrake and her car, a Honda Civic, slammed into the wreck, which mounted the pavement and got lodged in a Seville orange tree. It was a good thing it went sideways, because if it went straight ahead, it would have crashed into Sotiria's old car, a few meters away. I came down with sleep in my eyes, and while the neighbours were prying loose that silly cow's car, I parked Sotiria's car under our block of flats.

It was three o'clock when I went upstairs and stepped out onto the balcony to smoke and have the coffee which my wife had prepared in the meantime. Across the street, that blonde twig was saying to her wanker husband–both of them professors believe it or not– "How did the handbrake got loose on its own?" That's when Sotiria came up with an awesome idea and once more, I had to hand it her. We talked about it and the next day at noon she called the professor:

"This is Mrs. Achtidis, from across the street. I took my car to work in the morning and I noticed the temperature rising. I took it to the auto repair shop and they told me that the radiator was damaged in yesterday's crash and that the engine almost blew out."

"What the heck are you saying? My car crashed into the abandoned car and not your car, which was five meters away," said the nitwit.

"And yet, the wreck crashed into my car and broke my radiator," said Sotiria.

"What are you talking about? The Volkswagen is still pinned to the tree. It didn't even touch your car, it was five meters away," she insisted.

"It was dark and you couldn't see well, ma'am. You have to write me a statement, otherwise I will make a claim against you," my missus said angrily.

"You better write her a statement or you'll have me to deal with, you tart!" I shouted from inside the house.

"Alright, if you think you're entitled to compensation, I will write it," said the literature–God help us–professor. It's plonkers like them who teach our children how to read and write and have brought this country to the mess it's in.

And so once more, thanks to Sotiria's wits and my roughness, we pocketed three hundred euros.

Chapter 48

But three hundred euros in compensation wasn't going to cut it. They vanished into thin air within a week and the situation at home deteriorated. Sotiria went back to sulking and Nickie told me "Strato dear, go suck an egg," when I told her to do her homework.

On Saturday afternoon I ran into Memos in the square.

"What's up, Stratos, we haven't seen you lately!" he said and bought me a whisky.

"Did you get your hands on Anna's stash again?" I winked at him.

"No, it's my money," said Memos.

"How come?" I looked at him in disbelief.

"I finally managed to get myself a pension, brother," Memos said and showed me his wallet. One whisky became two and then three, and at about ten thirty, Stathogiannis showed up.

"Hey, brother. How are you?" he asked.

"Good," I said and avoided looking at the jaw I had smashed up.

"Let's buy you a drink," Memos said.

He sat opposite from me, lit a cigarette and we toasted to our health. His jaw was trembling. It was the first time I got a good look at the deformity I had given him.

"Forgive me, my brother," I said sorrowfully.

"You're forgiven," he said and hugged me. I hugged him back. Blood is thicker than water.

After that we started talking about chicks and school and how Smaras had made us orphans. Time passed and I got up to leave.

"Already? Why don't you come with us to a sleazy bar in Liosia?" Memos asked me. I checked the time and took another sip. For a second, Sotiria's angry face flashed before my eyes, but I quickly dismissed it. I wouldn't be Sotiria's plaything. No more slaves, no more, I thought. I emptied my glass and I heard myself say:

"Why not?"

We went out on the deserted road. Those two went ahead and I followed them under the impression I was zigzagging. We took Stathogiannis' Black Beauty and headed west and arrived in a neighbourhood without many lights, some place behind Lakiotis, in front of a narrow building with walls that stretched and shrank with a wild sound. Memos pushed open the door and I was immersed in the black hole. Dark as the night. "Too much darkness, my brother," I said, and the six whiskys I had gulped down earlier began to seethe inside me. I gazed in wonder at the black walls, the black loudspeakers hanging high above my head, blasting jet black music from their huge guts, the black stage and the black stairs with the silver handrail that went up and down alongside it. Memos helped me up a black stool.

"One Black & Decker" I said to the black-clad waitress before everything around me went dark. I ended up on the black floor with my mates hovering over me.

"What happened?" I asked.

"You probably fainted. You drank too much. Sit down for a minute," Stathogiannis said, but I jumped up like a spring and climbed onto the stage, where I started fondling the half-naked babes and dancing to whatever was playing; to Evdokia's *zei-bekiko*, to *Kitso's mother was sitting*... Jesus Christ, what was I doing at this sleazy place? After that I don't remember anything, except for Black Beauty's murmur through the hood and Sotiria's squeals, which ruined my mood.

"What did you do to him? Look at you, you toerag. You once again proved that you're nothing but a pig. I can't stand you anymore. Last time you swore on our children that you wouldn't put this shit in your mouth again and now look at you. Divorce! I want a divorce, can't take it anymore. Now get out of my house!" she blew her smoke in my face.

"You're kicking me out of my home, you bloody cunt? You leave if you don't like it. I'm not budging from here."

"That's what you think! Wait till I call 999," Sotiria grabbed the phone.

Defying Stathogiannis and Memos, who came between us, I lunged at her and snatched the phone, and after giving her a few slaps–she had it coming–I started smashing everything I could find. Then I lost control and started running with a broken beer bottle in my hand to slit the twat's throat, but I slipped and landed on the sofa. I felt something salty oozing out of my mouth, a paralysis and the world spinning around me. I fell asleep scared.

Sunday noon we had a family meeting; me, Sotiria, and our mothers. Mrs. Nickie feigned ignorance and Sotiria's mother glared at me.

"Be a little patient, my child, and everything is going to be alright," my mother begged Sotiria, and when she saw that she wasn't backing down, she turned and said to Katina, who she used to mellifluously address with the formal "co-mother-in-law": "Get your daughter and the children, and get out. It's Stratos' house. I mortgaged my house in order to get him the loan."

"Where is she going to go with two underage kids, co-mother-in-law? All these years, she is been putting up with your sonny, the drunkard, who has managed to destroy everything except for the walls. Tonight, he nearly slaughtered her. He needs to get a grip before it's too late for all of us," Katina took a stand.

"I didn't know that," my mother started whimpering.

"How did you not know, Mrs. Nickie?" Sotiria jumped in. "You don't have enough fingers and toes to count the times when, alerted by the neighbourhood, you came here in the middle of the night to collect him. On the nights I work, your Stratos puts the stereo at full blast–I wish you'd never bought him that thing–and smashes empty beer bottles on the street. Did you forget how a few years back you were on your knees pleading with him to turn down the damn thing? He was playing at full blast and everyone on Olofitou had to listen to Terlegas nonstop? The neighbours called 999. Stratos didn't let them in and so they left. Like they would stay and try to tame your beast. By the time you arrived and got him to turn it off, every block of flats in Labrini was lit up. You think I wouldn't find out? I also have people in the neighbourhood who keep me in the loop. I felt sorry for you at the time and didn't bring it up. She's a mother, I thought, she must be sick of her son's actions."

"If you saw all that, Sotiria dear, why did you let him knock you up second time around?" said my mother, shaking.

"Keep your hands off my Nikolakis!" Sotiria rushed toward her, and if Nickie wasn't there to start screaming, she would have pulled out every hair from my mum's head, hairs that hairspray barely held fast to her skull. Poor mum.

"I'm determined not to give him another chance. Stratos will leave home for good. He drove my first child mad, I won't let him turn the second one, and me with him," Sotiria said and thereby got rid of me, like shaking an insect off her collar.

Chapter 49

They came into my home at dawn. Three of them. They were dressed in grey camouflage uniforms, identical to the ones worn by the Hellenic Commando Unit for morning routine. I reached for the remote control to turn off the TV that had been playing since Sotiria left with the children and her mother. One of them twisted my arm.

"Easy, man," I tried to stifle the groan that wedged between my teeth.

They told me to cut the crap and stand up. They were taking me to the police station.

"Why, man? I'm not drunk, the stereo is off and I didn't do anything."

"The officer will explain," they said and they forced me up.

They pushed me into the police car. The light on the corner lamppost went out. It was chilly, it would soon be daylight. Dessie's dog from across the street growled. Until we reached the station, I didn't make a peep. They led me up to the second floor. The duty officer was sitting on his desk. Smoke rose from the ashtray next to him.

"Well, look who's here?" he said with a killer smile.

"Good eve... Good morning, Officer," I said.

He looked me sternly in the eye, I remember, and announced to me that Sotiria had won a restraining order and that I was not to set foot in her home until the children were of age.

"What are you saying, Officer? She kicked me out of my own flat? Me? When I sweated blood to get it? I'm still paying off the mortgage; it's in my name."

"Whether it's in your name or not, if you so much as go near the door, before your son turns eighteen, you'll be arrested. That's the law."

I suddenly felt tired. I went numb and a lump rose in my throat. I slumped into the chair across from him and allowed him to stare at me like I was a worm. I felt like a worm. The woman of my life had given me to the coppers, I was at their mercy. I didn't even have the strength to talk, let alone stand up. I had indeed come a long way. And how much farther could I have gone, being the son of a drunkard, the grandson of a bully and the third grandson of a killer? I spent a lifetime with three stamps branded onto my forehead. Before we buried my father, the neighbours asked me with their eyes and mouths: "Did your father drink again tonight? Did he beat up your mother?" and I prayed for the earth to open up and swallow me. And my grandfather was three times as bad as his son and my father. I couldn't wipe from my mind the image of grandfather Stratos chasing after my mother with a razor in the yard and then the officer with that billy club pushing him into the room and their yells that carried down to the lower field, and then, hours later, finding him in his bed with his head buried in the red shag rug! I was born in shit, I grew up in shit, I couldn't go any lower than that.

My mother, alerted by the officer, came to collect me. From the look on her face, I realised that it was over and done with. She told me to come to the house and I replied that I would go there in the evening. I had to gather my stuff. I arrived at my childhood home with a suitcase, a black rubbish bag and such a trembling that I couldn't insert the key in the lock. I had been sober for two days.

The smell of spinach pie came through the door. "You make the best pies, mother. There isn't a woman who can hold a candle to you," I said to her.

She looked at me under the cooker hood and bit her lip which etched her wrinkly lips. You have grown old mother, I pondered, and sat on the chest bed behind the round table.

"You want coffee?" she asked me dryly.

"I do, mum," I said. "Now we're starting all over just the two us."

She came over, sat beside me and put her arms around me. We both cried buckets.

Next day I woke up in my old life and I found it difficult to remember what had happened. All those years spent away from my childhood room now seemed like a dream. The sun came through the blinds and fell on my pillow. The air I breathed smelled of mothballs. All these years and you still can't part with those, mother, I thought, you're going to drown us in mothballs.

"Don't push, there's plenty to go around."

From Irakliou came the voice of Mr. Stelios who owned the, whatchamacallit, Katerina Supermarket. Good thing he hadn't named it "Stelios, the Bald Boy." I opened the shutters and went out onto the balcony to light a cigarette.

"Don't push, there's plenty to go around," I heard Mr. Stelios say again.

"Why are you shouting, old chap, and bursting our eardrums? There's no customers!" I called out to him but I stopped talking when I saw three men dressed in brown clothes slipping into the basement. They said something to Mr. Stelios and he started swearing. Shortly after, I saw them run out. One of them tripped on the last of the three steps that led down to the shop and the chief chased after them with a machete.

"Damn you, you bastards, for coming in first thing in the morning to do a check on me. If you ever come around here again, I will kneecap you and I will come up and tear down your sewer, you punks; when all you do is accept bribes or impose taxes!"

"Amen to that, Mr. Stelios, you hero. The neighbourhood won't put up with revenue officers," I shouted, and went down to Paranda to get a coffee.

Chapter 50

Regardless of one's attempts to fix things, they follow their course and once they go askew it's hard to get them straightened out. You have to rip out and rebuild from scratch a roof that has even one crooked beam, you can't patch it up. The same was true for me; it all went south from the time I was born and, in spite of my best efforts, it wasn't going to straighten out. I did the math and realised that at forty-two I was skint, and at a critical time no less, with not much room for faulty manoeuvring.

I had cut ties with Taratselis and missed out on all those nice day wages he gave me every now and then. No wheels came by the Tsunami, and Lola wouldn't even glance my way. My daughter ignored me, my son cried and didn't want to be separated from me on Sunday evenings when I drove him home, as the judge ordered, and my wife–I don't even want to talk about her. My brother would ride his bike drunk and disappear God knows where in the afternoons, and the furrow between my mother's eyebrows grew deeper every day. And then, to add insult to injury, this happened:

That day I was changing the oils of a neighbour's Renault, who didn't know which way to open the bonnet, and I got fifty euros. Around noon I went straight to IZO, where I found Stathogiannis and Memos.

"How are you doing, man?" they asked me simultaneously and I spilled out my troubles to them.

"Why did you go and pick a fight with Taratselis? Now with the crisis and everyone going apeshit for a day's wage, I would beg him to bone my mother. Find a way to get on his good side again. I saw him tailing your aunt again. Old loves die hard. Let her intervene to reconcile you too, so we can get some food in you, brother," Stathogiannis advised me with his mouth full.

I ordered Ouzo Mini, neat, when that bugger, Simos showed up.

"Mate, hey mate, are you going to buy me a shot?" he said and wiped his snot with the back of his sleeve. I was disgusted.

"Sod off, you son of a bitch," I raised my hand against him.

"Leave him be. What's it to you?" Stathogiannis said.

"He bothers me. I feel nauseous just looking at him."

"Come on now, why are you like that?" Simos said with tears streaming down his face.

"Sod off, or I'll start calling you names," I snapped.

"Is that so? Shame on you for badmouthing me, when I slaved at your shop for a year without getting a penny."

"You still can't count, eh? There are nine months from March to November, not a year. As for money, I never hired you to pay you. Sakis was my employee. You used to come in, I fed you, I watered you, I bought you cigarettes and, as a thank you, you drove away my customers. Get out of here or it's going to get messy."

"I will, but by nightfall I'll show you who you are dealing with."

I lunged to beat him up, but he got out in time, dragging that bloody leg of his. I ordered a fourth ouzo, but couldn't get it down. Something stuck in my throat. That no-good cripple, that retarded bastard had ruined my day. I left at seven with a weight on my chest.

The afternoon was warm, July was in full swing. At the junction of Irakliou and Saint Lavras, I noticed three fire engines going into Saint Antoniou. I rush over and what do I see? Smoke and flames coming out of the Tsunami and my mother and her sister in the street in a frantic state. The firemen struggled to open the fire hydrant and through the rickety garage doors they pour tons of water and foam into the shop, since lubricants are flammable.

An hour later they managed to put out the fire. It was a complete destruction. Fortunately, my mother's house was spared. I was left staring at the walls in silence. The fireman asked me who could have thrown a lit oakum in the lubricants and I couldn't make sense of anything. Then my mother said that she had seen Simos snooping around the garage door, but she hadn't given it another thought.

Simos had found the key he knew I left on top of the roller shutter, opened the garage door and started the fire. Stratos was now clinically dead. There was no resurrection for Stratos. I asked my mother for fifty euros and came back eight days later in very bad shape. I don't even remember what I did in those eight days. I don't know how I survived. Nor do I know who among the people who fell into my hands during those wild days made it through. I became a wild beast.

Chapter 51

The time that followed was spent drinking, smoking, and hanging out with Dimitris. I no longer went up to the square or to IZO. I didn't want to see my friends. I didn't feel like going even as far as Smaras' grave, which is a stone's throw away from my childhood home, to light him a cigarette and tell him about my suffering. I was ashamed. I was ashamed of my empty pockets, my empty life, of everything I had lost. Lefteris was apathetic, as always. Only mother always waited for me with food on the table, arms open wide and tears in her eyes. Oh, mum, you're the most precious thing in my life.

This time it was full-blown fall and things didn't look promising. The shop was trashed and there was no hope of restoring it, since it wasn't insured and the nutcase who had burned it down was in a mental hospital, but even if he wasn't, he couldn't afford to reimburse me. I started to relapse, when God took pity on me and, with Dimitris' intervention, I was hired as a driver in a taxi company with good pay and commission on the fares. And so I went back to routine. Ten to twelve hours a day I laboured in Athens in an annoying job, a job not for the faint of heart, which I wasn't anyway. Drive, neutral, drive, exhaust fumes and a full bladder. There is no greater torture than the torture of taxi drivers; wanting to pee yet being stuck in traffic. Ten months went by and, having met with plenty of weird incidents and crazy people, we made to the summer. I usually lined up outside Helena maternity hospital.

That night was slow until two o'clock when I was approached by a hunched-up lady pulling one of those fabric-covered shopping carts old ladies use to put groceries in. Mrs. Nickie has one just like that.

"Will you take me, lad, to the Three Bridges?" she asked me.

"I will, ma'am," I said and opened the boot to load her cart.

"This I will take with me," she pulled the cart close to her.

"No way, ma'am. This taxi is deluxe and luggage goes in the boot," I said, and reached for her shit.

"But I can't leave it in the back. My wallet's in there."

"Take your wallet with you, but the cart goes in the back. The taxi is deluxe," I repeated. Stratos had experience with cleaning cars, and wouldn't budge on such matters. He had set up a full-fledged Tsunami, after all.

With her hand locked on the handle of her cart, the old lady stared at the road, alternately looking at me and the open boot. The silver plate on my watch gleamed in the weak moonlight. It was already ten past two, I couldn't stand her any longer.

"Listen now," I said to her. "I'm not putting you in the taxi the way you want to. I'll turn you over to the next one," and I whistled to Stelios, who rushed to pick her up. I wasn't fool enough to put that crazy wrinkly and her dusty cart in my shining car for a mere fifteen euros.

As soon as Stelios' taxi, an old Nissan Sunny, a '95 model, was out of sight, I sat on the bench in the square and started talking to my third-in-line colleague Mr. Alekos, about chicks and night clubs and about the whores of Iera Odos and the old days, when the taxi business was a goldmine. It was three o'clock when Stelios returned.

"Fellas, beers on me tonight."

"Is it a special occasion, man, or did you become openhanded all of a sudden?"

"The old lady I took to the Three Bridges gave me a fifty and didn't want change for that."

"Well done!" I whistled, envious. "I'm in. Besides, you owe me. If I didn't hand her over, you wouldn't have gotten the fifty."

"I got the brown one for good behaviour. She wouldn't have given you a tenner, the way you treated her. That old woman who didn't look like much is a verger at a church and in her cart she had a great big bag with coins from the collection box, as well as fifties and a purple one, a dozen communion breads, oil from the saint's icon and a bottle of holy water. She sprinkled holy water on me and the car, inside and out, and gave me the brown one, because I accepted her wishes."

I was awestruck.

Chapter 52

Mrs. Nickie always told me: "Be careful how you talk, because you never know who you're dealing with." I couldn't believe my ears about the verger lady, but I didn't say anything, instead I gutted the can of Coca-Cola which was in front of me, next to the dumpster. We lounged on the bench under the trees and there was a yellow, sickly moon. Come four o'clock, the shadows of the trees turned askew, and the moon leaned behind the hospital's roof. Not a soul out on the street, no money tonight. We lit a cigarette and about half an hour later–no use waiting longer–we got into the cars and drove down to Liosion, to a local owned by the two women, that never closes. Nela, from Georgia, cracked open three Amstels with the key that hangs around her neck and bumps into her tits as she tramps. One night I had shoved my head into those titties and I shagged her in the bathroom. Nela placed the bottle in front of me and as the foam spilled from its cold neck licking the gold Amstel logo, I chugged it to cool myself down.

"Ahh..." I blurted out with my eyes fixed on the furrow between her tits. I couldn't control myself. I asked for a second bottle.

"Cheers to us." Stelios, Mr. Alekos and I all clinked our bottles; it was my second drink and their first. Nela cuddled up to me. She warmed me even more, but I liked it. Soon I clinked my fourth bottle with my colleagues. I couldn't resist beer the way it made its way down my throat, foamy and cold, and exploded in my stomach like those volcanoes in Manila with the young tarts that the lawyer had told me about.

That old lawyer I picked up from the airport a few days earlier, who came straight from the Philippines, had told me that for one euro, you get ten-year-old mouths sucking your dick, and for two, they let you stick your erect dick up their ass, and it's like sticking it in butter, and you cum, you cum nonstop. "This is what I call a shagging," said the old geezer who saves up his pension in order to go shag little kids ten days a year. I was repulsed. "That's the only place where I get a hard-on," the old bastard continued, and half-heartedly handed me my thirty euros, the cheapskate. Naturally I had slightly tampered with the taximeter and that way I got my revenge on him. It wasn't a big deal, I got about ten euros extra from that disgraceful paedophile–and needless to say, I didn't go out to take his suitcase out of the boot. I made him pull it out with his filthy hands and when he managed to set it on the pavement, I revved up and left, emptying the exhaust fume on him making the sleazeball look like a Filipino himself, which he did anyway.

The sun was coming up and the table was filled with empty beer bottles.

"Time to go," said Stelios.

I got up willingly, but everything was spinning, while Svetlana's, not Nela's, pallid face broadened and was blocking my way to the door. I remember slumping down in the chair, that bounced, its dry sound ruining the beauty of my fall.

"You're plastered, man," I heard Stelios next to me.

"Nela, make him one, neat."

"No, no, I don't want coffee," I squealed. I threw my head on the table and listened to the bottles crashing and falling on the concrete. It was deafening.

"Come, have a coffee," said Svetlana in broken Greek. I turned to look at her. "Drink it," she said and the teeth of her upper dentures appeared menacing.

"No," I said and knocked the rest of the bottles over. I heard a commotion around me and Nela talking to Stelios and Mr. Alekos. I didn't want any distractions from my drunken stupor.

"I can't keep him. Look what he did, I have to clean up in order to open at ten. I won't have time to rest," said the Russian.

"In that case, why didn't you kick us out, all this time?" Mr. Alekos said.

"If there's work, I keep the place open. He has stopped drinking now. I haven't opened up a beer in over half an hour."

"It'd be better if you get him to nap in the little room in the back you keep for emergencies."

"No one goes in there unless he pays fifty euros, and Stratos is broke."

That bloody whore, that frigging Russian. I've been paying her all this time and I need her this one time and she kicks me out because I am poor.

"Come on, man, let's go. Come, your wife will be waiting up," Stelios nudged me.

"I have no wife; I have no kids. The wife thing is over."

I saw her in the back of my mind, with her arms open to greet me in front of the door to our block of flats and I started tearing up.

"Come on, man. Hang in there."

I got up with difficulty. The shithole quaked around me and my legs couldn't hold me up. "*I don't pretend I'm a saint, oh, I loved, I don't pretend to be a saint, oh, I sinned...*" the song rumbled up from my lungs and turned into coughing and vomiting.

"You turned this place into a dump!" Nela shouted and raised a mop against us.

"Get your shit together," Stelios said to her and cleaned my face with a towel that reeked of fish.

"Get your shit together or else," I tried to tell her too. She looked at me with those sleepy eyes which resembled a drizzled pavement. I felt sick and I burped.

The light coming in bright over the rooftops of the blocks of flats to the east blinded me like the light reflected in the eyes of the blackbirds lying in the foliage of the trees in Antista. Ah, my poor blackbirds, I loved it when I woke you up with the flashlight and I loved it when Uncle Nikiforos knitted button holes with his buckshot on your gray bodies.

Stelios, with the help of Mr. Alekos, escorted me to the car. It took me half an hour to find the keys and I thought that the passenger's door was that of the driver's. I was bladdered, bladdered as fuck. I tried to get in and fell flat on my back on the street.

"Damn you. You even changed my driver's door today," I cursed.

A man makes a mistake once and has one too many drinks and the world shifts and transforms around him to punish him for his courage to live, even for just one night, above the ground that impatiently waits to swallow us all. Whoever tries to escape, will be tortured for his fearlessness, that which prudent men call a misstep. Fuck them all. I try to get up while remaining calm.

"Come here, hey, come here, man," I hear Stelios in my ear. "You're not getting into the car, you're bladdered. I will take you home and notify the company to send here your replacement to pick up your car."

"I'll take it with me," my voice sounded hoarse, unrecognisable.

"Don't act tough. If you take it, it will take control, and you'll probably take innocent lives that happen to be in your way."

From what I recall, I didn't lay down my arms, but rather moved again towards the door, which opened above my head as I was crawling on the concrete. However, when I realised that I really couldn't manage it, I let Stelios pull me into his own taxi.

I still don't want to remember the tears my mother shed seeing me, or how she changed my clothes and put me to bed.

Chapter 53

After that, I spent three whole months without going out. And then things went sour.

I was driving on Patission, when I picked up an old man.

"We're going to Koukaki," he said. I switched on the meter and drove off.

"We will take Alexandras," he instructed.

"How can we get to Koukaki via Alexandras, mister?" I asked.

"I will tell you. I want us to avoid the traffic on Patission."

He took me through some narrow streets and some stop signs, grinding my gears. After going by Kolonaki and getting stuck in traffic, we arrived at Koukaki.

"Pull over here. What do I owe you?"

"Twenty euros."

"Patission to Koukaki, twenty euros?"

"Well, you had me driving around Athens to get here."

"You're a thief!" he shouted.

"You are one to talk!" I replied.

"Here's five, which is more than enough." He tossed me a fiver.

"Up yours. Give me twenty and I'll go," I exclaimed.

"If you get more than five euros, I'll eat my hat," he said and opened the door.

"Where do you think you're going, pops?" I pulled the hand-brake.

"Don't you dare call me pops, or I'll fuck your place up, you bastard," he said and threw a wrinkled fiver in the front seat.

"Wait a second. If you want to fuck my place up, let me give you the keys!"

I got out of the car in a state of frenzy. I caught up with him in the corner and beat him up badly. Some bystanders were shouting: "Leave the man alone!" but I made sure he was hospital material. Afterwards I got in the taxi and left.

A couple of days later, my boss called me in to tell me to leave and wait for a summons to appear in court. The old man was in intensive care. Luckily, I hadn't been caught in flagrante delicto. I left angry. Two years in that shitty job was a long time.

Chapter 54

"Mum, I'm out of work again," I said to Mrs. Nickie as I entered the kitchen. She looked up. She raised her eyes on me and it was as if she couldn't see me.

"Don't you have anything to say?" I asked her.

"What is there to say, Stratos? That I have bet on the wrong horse?" her words stabbed me where it hurt the most.

From that day on, my life flatlined. I locked myself in my room with the shutters ajar, so that the light comes in without having to squint. Mrs. Nickie pleaded with me to take a shower and eat. The only thing that kept me going was Nikolakis who waited for me eagerly to go pick him up first thing on Saturday mornings. We would go to the swings, to the zoo, to Goody's and the parkland to chase after the cats that twats like Dessie round up to feed.

In August, Nikolakis vacationed at his grandmother's, Katina. He came back at the end of the month and I took him the first weekend of September. We went everywhere during those days–to the amusement park, to Porto Rafti for swimming, to the souvlaki joint and to every single swing in the neighbourhood. Come Sunday night, I rang Sotiria's door. The door opened, but the child didn't want to go up.

"Come up!" his mother shouted over the intercom.

"I want my daddy," Nikolakis clung onto my legs.

"Go," I said to him and I cried and he clung to me even more. "Go, child."

"No, I want you with me in our house. Come upstairs, daddy, and we can sleep on the sofa in each other's arms, like we used to, and I'll introduce you to Phoebus, our doggy."

"I don't like dogs," I said.

"If you don't like him, I'll throw him off the balcony, as long as you come and stay with us. I want you near me forever."

"He's not coming up!" I yelled towards the balcony.

Sotiria wasn't saying anything. Five minutes passed, ten minutes, Nikos wouldn't budge. Then the door opened and Sotiria came out. She was gorgeous. I hadn't seen her in three whole months. She didn't talk to me; she didn't even look at me. I started to leave and Nikolakis came after me, crying.

"I want my daddy," he shouted.

I ran out, but his crying followed me all the way to the avenue. I went through the cemetery and when I arrived outside my house, I headed back. I headed up to the square and went straight to the ouzerie and got hammered.

Chapter 55

It's been almost three years from the day I got back to my child-hood home, in my old neighbourhood and to Mrs. Nickie's nag-gings. "Don't move from the sofa until the floor dries", "Put the toilet seat up when you pee", "Don't eat standing up." Even the walls couldn't bear her nagging, but I didn't hold it against her. I had put her through a lot, poor woman.

So, I once more swallowed my pride and went to Stathogiannis this time.

"I got nothing, but why don't you go to the HVAC technician across the street? I heard he needs a man for installing air condi-tioners. Blocks of flats don't use petrol anymore, and anyone who still has money buys air conditioners," he said.

Accordingly, I got a job at 'Cooling-Heating, Eftychia'. The pay was good and the job was a piece of cake for someone like me, who had climbed on every rooftop in Athens. I worked nonstop for two months. Home-work, work-home, and then bed. I saved up some money and got my act together again. I started going to the football field with Stathogiannis and to IZO for beers. Now and then, for a change, I would visit the guys at Black Dog.

And right when I got my act together, I started thinking about women again. It's common knowledge that a man can't live without a woman. It's not just the pressing matter of shagging. It's about the touch, the morning greeting, the going out, the freshly washed jeans, the flat smell on your hair after a night with a chick, it's so many things that God made and won't change, despite the efforts of feminists, who are a bunch of no-good spinsters with moustaches and unshaved legs and armpits, that even a tom cat wouldn't go near. There is nothing more disgusting than unshaved female armpits.

On weekends, therefore, I went to Paranda and started ogling Lola again, who systematically avoided me.

"What's it going to be, Lola love? When are we going to drink again that good old coffee of ours?" I couldn't help but say to her one day.

"She looked at me absentmindedly, the way that says *I don't know, pardon me, who are you sir*?

"Don't act like you don't understand. I was thinking that since I am alone, you're alone, we can meet up at your house and see if this thing works: me, you and your children," I insisted.

"If you think I'm going to let you into my house, you've got another think coming. Do you forget that you left me high and dry? Do you forget that I begged to see you and you avoided me like the plague? Did you ever ask how it was for me after our breakup, the tears I shed and my sorrow? And you remember me now that your wife kicked you out, but it's too late, that ship has sailed my friend. If you want a coffee, you'll pay," she said and leaned over to clean the counter in front of me with a Wettex, looking me straight in the eye.

I flew off the handle and knocked both the coffee cup and the glass of water onto the floor, breaking them into a thousand pieces.

"Now pick them up; it serves you right. Stratos may give presents, but he never paid nor he will ever pay for a shag," I said and left without paying.

Chapter 56

After my quarrel with Lola, Black Dog became my second home. I went down there almost every afternoon for a freddo cappuccino or cold beers, depending on the weather and my disposition. The attic was packed at all hours and everyone had his own spot. I always sat close to the window. I loved to watch the trains going back and forth with their soothing sound–"clap, clap, clap"–from dawn to midnight. Dimitris carried a lot of weight in there. He would come in and nearly everyone would get up to greet him. No one made a sound when he presented the organisation's secret action plans, or made his political statements. Who would have thought that an illiterate plonker like himself, and with the kind of troubles he had with the underground in his youth, would hold such a position.

There, at the table, I drank and chatted with the guys in the black clothes and the Greek-themed tattoos. I can't say I agreed with them on everything, but when everyone else had turned their backs on me, they made me feel like I belonged somewhere, like I was somebody, which made it easy to ignore their ideologies and the manner in which they asserted their beliefs. I didn't think more of it. I didn't delve deeper. Being there was a good thing.

Generally speaking, I had decided not to object to the things I heard, and I didn't take a stand when they kicked out a Pakistani man who sold flowers and made the mistake of coming up to the attic.

"You should have known better!" I said to him and on my way out, stepping on his flowers, that were scattered across the stairway.

Apart from that, although I was pressured to join their operations which I had so far shunned, they were stand-up guys, who had supported me and continued to support me whenever I needed them.

Chapter 57

After Lola rejected me, I lowered my standards and made a pass at Jenny when I bumped into her a few days later at the bus stop.

"Hello, Jenny, how's it going?"

"Fine," she said and her mouth opened like a cesspit.

"Are you waiting for the bus?"

"No, a taxi. I'm going down to Victoria, where you-know-who is waiting for me." "Who's that?"

"Who else? Taratselis."

"And what is Mister Nikos doing down there?"

"Well, last Christmas I made it clear to him: 'If you want to shag, it's only in a hotel from now on. I have been freezing my ass off at the quarries and construction sites'. At first, he played hard to get, but I didn't care that much, since I had the doctor. But before the week was out, he begged me to go find him in a five-star hotel."

"What's on your schedule for later? Maybe you'd like to grab a coffee with me?" I asked her that but it felt like I was just going through the motions.

"I don't have time for more coffees. The doctor and Taratselis suffice. They're enough," said Jenny and signalled a taxi which came to an abrupt halt in front of her.

"Bye," she said with her wide-opened mouth and slumped in the back seat. She told the driver to head to Victoria and they vanished into thin air.

I went through the roof. Disgusted, I spat on the pavement and went up the street to Cooling-Heating, Eftychia. Oh, Stratos, look what you've been reduced to. Being rejected by Jenny. Jenny, of all people!

I walked into the shop in a bad mood. It was June and it was really warm. I ordered an iced coffee and sat at the desk, when the phone rang.

"Come quickly, come. The air conditioner broke down and the girls are getting hot!" the customer said.

"What's wrong with it?" I asked.

"We press the remote control and it won't start."

I wrote down the telephone and the address on a piece of paper and took it to my boss, who was repairing a motor in the back of the shop.

"It doesn't have to be me. You can go and check it out. They're probably out of batteries. Get some batteries and a new remote control. Turn on the machine, pretend you're fixing it, then test the remote control. If it starts, get seventy euros and leave. If it's because of something else, let me know," said the boss.

I took the company's van and got off at Academia Platonos. I walked through some narrow streets lined with dilapidated houses, until I reached Erifilis and Andromeda. Above the iron door, there was a red light. I look at the number, I look at my notepad. I had been called to a brothel! I walk in and bump into a fat lady.

"Welcome!"

"I came for the air conditioner."

"And here I thought you were a client."

"Where's the machine?"

"This way," she said and opened a door. The hooker was on top of a bald fat man who was left with his mouth hanging open.

"It's the guy for the air conditioner," the Madam made the introductions.

"Come, come," said the hooker. "You, put this on," she threw her robe to the fat man, who was at a loss.

I was stuck in the doorway.

"Come on in, love, we won't hurt you. Here's the patient. It won't start," said the hooker stark naked under the air conditioner.

"I need a ladder," I tried not to look at her, sickened from inhaling the sour smell of shag.

The Madam ran to get me one.

I climbed up and I did exactly what my boss had said. Then I secretly changed the remote control's batteries and the machine started.

"Well done, lad," said the Madam.

"Keep it up and good luck," I went out and closed the door behind me. The hall was empty.

"Ma'am, ma'am!" I called out.

"I'm here," her voice came from the kitchen.

"Ready. It will be seventy euros."

"I don't have money."

"And how am I going to get paid?"

"It's too early and we haven't made any money. You can wait a while to put it together, unless you want to be paid in kind."

"Thank you, ma'am, but no thanks. I'm an employee and I have to take the money to the boss."

"In that case, sit down and wait for her inside to finish," the Madam pointed to the sofa behind the kitchen table that was covered in hair from the cat that had begun to rub against my legs.

"Collect your cat, or I'll kick her."

"If you harm Semiramis, I'll twist your balls," the Madam yelled.

I told her to give me my money so I could leave, or I'd turn that shithole into a shithole. She hastily paid me–apparently, I had crazy eyes. And she had money–plenty of it–in a coffee can. Actually, I took an extra fifty euros from her for my trouble and my emotional distress, and I left. I started the engine, but before I could make a run for it, the Madam and a copper jumped me and dragged me out by force. They took me down to the station for theft but they let me out that night.

I got back to the shop at ten o'clock. The boss had made calls everywhere. I told him what had happened and he told me to pack my things and leave. He didn't want to be associated with crooks. The crook called me a crook.

Chapter 58

I was out of a job again and with another court case hanging over my head.

"Did you take a work leave?" my mother asked me.

"Yes, mum."

I didn't want to give her grief. I stayed home for a week and in the mornings, I went to Parada for coffee. Lola wouldn't as much as look at me, she had Koula bring me my coffee. I couldn't bear her contempt and the thought that she was an Albanian was all the more reason for making my blood boil. The tail wagging the dog; what's that about? This is the state I was in when uncle Nikiforos came.

"What's wrong with my nephew?" he asked.

I opened my heart to him. Nikiforos, my father's brother, had left the village when he was young to go to Athens, where he got mixed up with a man who gave him a deckhand job on a ship doing the route Piraeus-Morocco. And though he used to be destitute, he all of a sudden showed up in Antista with money, gold teeth, new, soft white shoes and gold watches, in the company of a gorgeous babe named Afro, who wore a mini skirt and a white blouse stamped with two huge red lips and a fresh tongue sticking out–the Rolling Stones' logo, as I later found out. Everyone was going on about his success and grandfather Stratos was proud as a peacock until they put him in jail for two years for drug trafficking.

When he got out, he married Afro, who had been waiting for him–because, mind you–the men of the Achtidis clan are good-looking. I will never forget that wedding, because it was the first time my mother talked to my grandfather after the death of my father. Afro arrived with her long veil trailing on the pavement and looking like a goddess. Afterwards we partied in a tavern down from Acharnon and I got plastered. It was the first time I got drunk. Afro stayed with Nikiforos for a year and then dumped him.

When he was in his forties, uncle took in Katinitsa, a lame spinster from Patissia with a house and a bus, and a tricycle on top. Katinitsa had fingers like sausages and she walked like a boat in a storm. She also had five or six childless uncles who left her their legacies, so that with Nikiforos, she could splurge the money on nightclubs and the good life. That's how Nikiforos spent his life, alternating between ships, dance floors, the streets and jail.

"You want money, nephew?" my uncle asked me and pulled out a green one. I took it.

"Would you like to get five grand more?" he said and feigned an absent look towards Irakliou.

"Is there a blind man who doesn't want to see?" I replied.

"Come round the house tomorrow night and I'll tell you about it," he said.

So, I did. I went there, I talked with him and one week later we made our first trip to Albania. I put in the car, he put in the brains and the petrol, and after spending three days behind the wheel I came home with five grand. As easy as that, that conniving Nikiforos turned me into a drug dealer, without me getting high myself, despite him saying to me "take as much as you need to get high for free."

We made two or three more such trips, until that day in Kakavia when they thought to search the car's tires and caught us red-handed. Police station, holding cell, fingerprints, car impoundment, in flagrante delicto. Then we were out again, without a penny to our name.

I made a call to Stathogiannis.

Chapter 59

Stathogiannis was waiting for me at the bus station in Kifissos, behind the wheel of Black Beauty.

"Hey, man," I said and slumped down next to him.

He started the car and without saying a word he took Kifissou, where there was heavy traffic. He then turned up Kaftatzoglou and instead of taking Patission, he went up on Galatsiou, then Protopapadaki and turned onto the ring road. It was a beautiful day outside, spring was almost over, summer was coming and the city was putting on its faded lukewarm colours. We went to Zeppelin and sat facing one another.

"Why are you acting this way, man?" Stathogiannis asked me with a dark look on his face. "Why are you tearing yourself apart? Why are you treating yourself like dirt and throwing yourself to the dogs? What is it that you don't have? You have your mother by your side, your children are well and you are still climbing the wall. Why is that? Why?"

"I don't know, I can't even think straight, man. I take this frigging life at face value and I keep on getting the short end of the stick. No matter what I do, no matter what I try to do, it goes to waste. I work in construction, houses are no longer built; I build the Tsunami, that bugger sets it on fire; I start a family, my wife gives me the boot; I drive a taxi, I get loonies for customers; I work with air conditioners, they kick me out; I try to help

Nikiforos, the coppers arrest me. Everything is wrong and I have neither the strength nor another opportunity to change anything," I replied and gazed down at Athens stretching out all the way to the glimmering sea.

"Of course, you can. Quit drinking and I'll put you in touch with a contractor who undertakes public works," he promised me.

"Drinking is my only consolation, but I'll try, man."

"Look here, Stratos, drinking makes some people brawl and become insensitive and other people cry like little girls. You belong to the first category. Drinking makes you violent, brings out the worse in you, it's not a good fit. Quit it already, so you can take it easy." He took a sip of his coffee and sat there gazing at the city.

We recalled the years when we used to play hooky from school, our promiscuities and our follies. Time passed and I was getting drowsy. It was around five o'clock when Stathogiannis paid the bill. We went down to Labrini, with 'Smoke on the water' playing at full blast. At the corner of Irakliou and Orfanidou, he turned on his hazard lights.

"You need anything else, mate?" he looked me in the eye.

"A twenty."

"Anything you want, brother."

I took it and got myself plastered, to forget.

Chapter 60

The following day was a bitter day. My mother was away. I got up after three o'clock feeling sad, thinking about my son and tearing up. In the afternoon I went down to Black Dog, where I met up with Dimitris and Lefteris. We were running an operation tonight, Dimitris told me. I asked him what kind of operation was he talking about and Lefteris told me not to ask questions and that I would soon find out. I didn't ask any more questions, I just hopped on Lefteris' bike. Besides, I didn't have anything better to do. Smaras was dead, I had lost touch with Memos, and Stathogiannis had a date with a chick he had been hanging out with lately.

"Be careful," I said to Lefteris on the way over, for he drove so fast that we nearly crashed into the rear end of every bus we encountered on Acharnon. We reached the beginning of Keramikos and parked the bike on the pavement outside a grey block of flats, next to about thirty other bikes. Dimitris dismounted and pushed the garage door upwards. We walked into a murky space, lit only by a little yellow light in the back, over a dark grey iron door.

"Today, you'll meet the leader," he said and pushed me into a black underground hall that reeked of manly odour.

Every Tom, Dick or Harry was in there. Some ugly looking guys, heavy-built, shaved heads with tattoos and muscles like bread loafs, were positioned to the left and the right of a platform.

The Black Dog gang was to my right, somewhere. They called us over, they had saved us seats. They were all talking loudly, the walls were pulsating. Suddenly there was silence. We could even hear our own breath, when a door opened and the leader stepped out onto the platform. He was short with glasses, dark-haired with protruding sparse teeth, he didn't look much of a leader to me. "Rise!" a metallic voice came from the back and they all jerked up and raised their hands like Hitler in the Reichstag.

"Get up, you prick," Lefteris nudged me and I got up reluctantly, since I hadn't yet sobered up from the previous night. The leader talked to us about the purity of the Greek race and how filthy the Bangladeshis were, but I noticed that he himself resembled a Bangladeshi in the way he looked and talked, rather than a purebred Greek, like he boasted. I wondered how his people didn't see it, but I didn't say anything, it was none of my business. After an hour of speeches and greetings, the leader requested volunteers for a covert operation. Lefteris said he was available, he said I was available too.

Around midnight, eight of us got into a black van parked in the second basement and Dimitris drove. After driving for half an hour, we stopped. They let us out and we walked down a street of broken pavements and rundown houses to our left and right, with broken windows and rickety roofs. A full moon hung over us. Dimitris signaled us to keep moving. We moved to the north silently and with caution, and at the first intersection we turned right and came across the thick shadow of a corner two-storey building. I felt my heart pounding in my chest like a drum. All this reminded me of my first training exercise in the Hellenic Commando Unit. We proceeded along the street and when we reached a dead end, we pushed open the last door. We entered a narrow space that smelled of piss, vomit, fart, and mould. I struggled not to puke my guts out. Carefully, we mounted a wooden staircase, which creaked with every wrong step.

When we reached the upper floor, someone turned on the flashlight shouting: "Everything that moves, gets slaughtered!"

We saw them lying one next to the other, fast asleep. "Rise!" came the same voice and I saw them jump up like blackbirds, unsuccessfully trying to make us out, given that the flashlight had blinded them. We jumped them and crushed their heads. Soon the place smelled of blood, piss, and faeces. I was the first to come down and I threw up in the corner.

Chapter 61

A new day dawns even in a cesspool. So, thanks to the guys, I was back on the street again, I became somebody and, most importantly, I felt useful in society. And since I had no one to answer to but Mrs. Nickie, I got back to drinking again.

"Thanks to you, the drill went very well," Dimitris told me at the Saturday night meeting and gave me a friendly pat on the back for my input in the attack at the south suburbs. I felt ten feet tall. It's no small feat to stand out in a group of purebred Greeks.

Early next Sunday morning, at four o'clock, I'm headed back to my childhood home tipsy and happy, when I change my mind and make a turn towards Olofitou.

I hide in Mrs. Dimitra's company car and the shadow of the Seville orange tree, that turns gloom into sheer darkness. I light a firecracker and I toss it at the wheels of Takis' BMW across the street. It's an inferno. The walls amplify the noise, and the car alarm which is set off is earsplitting. I slip into the adjacent parking lot and wait for the shutters to open so they can come out and see what's happened to their fish crates, whining and cursing at the bloody bugger who woke them up and threatening to call the police. Five minutes later the alarm stops. Not a peep, dead silence.

At twenty past four I throw the second firecracker, the explosion resounds, the car alarm sets off again. Not a soul. No one has the guts to go out to the balcony, like in the past, and call the police. Three years of austerity measures were enough to turn them from hotshots to jokes. They hide like rats in their burrows, trying to guess who it was behind their dark shutters and they wait, they wait for me; the one who is no longer afraid to face what he can become, not afraid to shed the blood of any frigging Asian who squeals like a hundred piglets. They wait for me to uncover them like a hedgehog and prune them. They know full well that their money, their houses, their children, their women, their honour and their bloody shitty lives are now in my hands and at my mercy.

www.ingramcontent.com/pod-product-compliance
Ingram Content Group UK Ltd.
Pitfield, Milton Keynes, MK11 3LW, UK
UKHW040956040925
462549UK00003B/3

9 781912 545520